12th Annual Kindle Book Awards
2023
Finalist
Young Adult
THE BEST OF INDIE
12th Annual Kindle Book Awards

Amazon Expert Reviewer:

"The writing is good...the plot is gripping"

Publisher's Weekly:

"...issues of race and identity are nicely handled"

Tough Times

by

Sheri McGuinn

Durare
Publishing

Bullhead City, AZ

www.sherimcguinn.com

smcguinn@sherimcguinn.com

sherimcguinn.substack.com

HUMAN
AUTHORED
AG Authors Guild
2687146

Table of Contents

RESOURCES

THANK YOU

BEHIND THE STORY & ACKNOWLEDGEMENTS

ALSO BY SHERI MCGUINN

DISCUSSION QUESTIONS

Wednesday: Tough Times

-1-

I should have been the first one home, not Missy. She was only seven. It was my job to protect her and Jimmy. I'd walked by their school to get them and then I took Jimmy to practice and brought Missy home, but not all the way. Right before we got to the apartments, Shenia Brown was out front of her house, almost like she was waiting for me. She smiled and said hey.

I just had to stop.

I'd been trying to get up the nerve to ask her to go out with me since the beginning of the year, when we both started tenth grade. Shenia is the prettiest girl I know. She has milk chocolate skin without a zit, shiny black ringlets kept short and natural, and the best smile in the world.

So when she said hey, I told Missy to head on home and show Mama her new paintings. I gave her my key because Mama always kept the doors locked.

Shenia and I had been talking on the phone about school stuff off and on for a month, so I was thinking she might like me a little, maybe enough to go out with me. I'd been practicing how I'd ask her for the last week. I meant for it to come out all smooth in the course of conversation, but instead I just blurted it out soon as I saw Missy go into the apartment.

"You wanna go walk in Old Town with me Saturday?"

"Maybe." Shenia smiled.

I grinned back at her, too stupid happy to say anything. Shenia could go out with anyone she wanted. Her boyfriend last summer was her big brother's Army buddy. He could treat her right. Any money I earned, I gave to Mama to help pay bills. So a Saturday walk in the old part of town was the best I could offer.

Shenia was saying how she liked the old boardwalks by the river when her cell jingled its pretty little tune. She checked to see who was calling, then gave it to me. "It's your phone."

Embarrassed, I explained, "We only have the one. I don't need it during the day."

I took her cell, "Mama?"

"Michael?" It was Missy.

That little girl's timing was lousy. Besides, Mama should be taking care of her now. I got her home. "What do you want, Missy?"

"Michael, Mama's gone."

She sounded scared, so I let go of my irritation and tried to make her feel better. "She probably went out for groceries. Or maybe she got a job interview. I'll be home in a few minutes. You're a big girl, just get a snack and turn on the TV."

"No, Michael. She's gone, like Betsy."

In the minute it took to get to Missy, my whole lousy life flashed through me, just like they say happens when you die.

Daddy was tall. I was four when he got knifed in a bar. He looked like a big waxy doll in the coffin. Mama couldn't stop crying. When we got home, our neighbor brought over some macaroni and cheese on a plate. She put it on the table and told me to sit.

"Your mama won't feel like cooking tonight. You eat this."

She went into the other room and sat down with Mama. I never have liked macaroni and cheese. I snuck close to where they were talking.

"I don't know what to do," Mama told her.

"What about your folks?"

"They never approved of Mike. They've barely spoken to me since Michael was born. They've never even seen him."

Mike McCarthy wasn't black Irish; he was just plain black as night. I came out the color of coffee with lots of cream in it and my kinky hair is auburn like Mama's. My grandfather, Michael Dolan, never saw me, but I got saddled with Michael Dolan McCarthy for my name.

"Families pull together in bad times. They'll help you out," said the neighbor.

Mama called her parents. Then she cried even harder. "They don't want anything to do with us."

"Because of a little color in your child? That's cold."

So I always knew it was my fault Mama's family wasn't there.

Lucky for us, Daddy's friend, Swede Johnson, loved kids.

He started coming by to spend time with me, and he fixed things around the house. He joked with Mama to cheer her up and he made her come along when he took me to the movies. When Swede got a job in Sacramento, we moved west with him.

He was as blonde as Daddy was dark, so Missy and Jimmy are both fair-skinned with white-blonde hair. But Swede always treated me like his oldest child. He taught me to play soccer and came to all my games, taught me how to work on cars and fix stuff around the house, taught me 'most everything I know. Summers we'd tube down the American River whenever it wasn't too wild for the little kids.

Mama laughed a lot when we were all together like that.

Then one day, Swede took me to a big gravel lot and taught me how to handle the car when it was skidding around. I couldn't believe he was letting me drive; I was only thirteen.

Then he told me how he'd waited too long to get that ugly old mole taken off the back of his neck. It was cancer, and it had already spread. He only had a few weeks.

"It's not fair!" I cried.

"Tough times make you stronger, Michael, as long as you don't lie around feeling sorry for yourself."

That's what he told me.

They'd been saving to buy a house, but medical bills took all of it. Swede was upset to be leaving things that way. But he helped Mama get herself a job, first one I remembered her having.

Swede died August sixth, my fourteenth birthday. He thought we'd be okay, and we were, for a little while.

I was going to play sports in high school—I'm an awesome soccer goalie and not too bad at basketball—but Mama worked until six every night. Jimmy was nine and too hyper to be on his own, let alone responsible for Missy, and Mama wasn't making enough for a sitter. We set it up for me to get out early every day so I could take care of the kids. Sometimes I'd take them over to the high school to watch soccer games, but the goalie was lousy and they kept losing. And Missy would complain she was tired and Jimmy never sat still.

Then in October, Mama got downsized. She called me into the kitchen and had me sit while she paced back and forth.

"I don't know what we're going to do, Michael."

"You'll get another job."

It didn't turn out that way. She got out there every day, putting in applications. I didn't try out for basketball—thought I'd have to quit when she started working again. But by spring unemployment ran out and we had to move into this ghetto apartment with two tiny bedrooms.

At first Missy slept in with Mama. Then Mama started going out at night. The next thing we knew, Missy was in our room on a cot and Lester was in with Mama. He helped with the bills, but I never liked him. I hoped he'd be gone once she got work again.

Then when summer came, I realized Mama still hadn't found a job because Lester worked nights and wanted her in bed with him during the day.

I only came home to eat and sleep. If she wanted someone to watch her kids, she could get up and do it herself.

On the Fourth of July, Lester worked for the holiday pay. When he finally left the apartment, I started helping Mama clear the table.

"I've got people five blocks around paying me to help with yard work," I bragged. "Soccer tryouts are in August. If I need to pay for anything, I'll be able to take care of it myself."

"I'm so proud of you," she said, and she pushed up her sleeves to wash the dishes.

I didn't say a word. I just stared at the purple finger marks on her forearms and clenched my jaw. My growth had started coming on and I probably would have killed that man if he'd been there at that moment. Mama didn't say anything, just pushed down her sleeves. She must've seen it in my eyes, though, 'cause she got his things together and put them by the back door before we left for the fireworks.

There were fireworks the next morning, too.

We were all still in bed when Lester used his key to come in and started screaming at Mama. I threw on my pants. Jimmy started to follow me.

"You stay with Missy," I told him.

Jimmy looked over and saw how tight our little sister was holding her stuffed dog. "Holler if you need help."

I ran down the hall to Mama's room. She was sitting on her bed in her nightgown. Lester had hold of her arm. I crossed that room in two steps and grabbed his wrist, hard.

"Get out!" The words came out of me in a growl.

"This is between your mama and me. Get back to your room."

I squeezed tighter and leaned into him. My other hand was in a fist, ready to fly. It was hard to hold back, but I knew it would mean more trouble if I didn't. Finally, he let go of Mama and broke away from my glare. I let him shake off my hand and stepped back.

He turned to her and said, "If I can't have you, nobody can."

"Don't you threaten her." I crowded his space again.

"You better watch your kids," he sneered on his way out.

That was back in July. Mama started looking for work again, but it seems like confident people get most jobs. Those bruises weren't the worst harm he did.

Then last week, our old calico cat got hit by a car.

Mama said animal control picked her up before I brought Jimmy home from soccer. Missy had seen the body, though, and cried until she fell asleep that night.

Mama kept telling her that Betsy had gone on to a better place.

Now Missy was telling me Mama was gone like Betsy.

Missy was sitting at the top of the stairs, her hands together tight on her pinched knees. Her eyes were twice their normal size. She looked like one of those little china dolls people collect, only scared.

"Where is she?" I shouted.

She pointed to Mama's bedroom with her chin. I took the stairs three at a time, thinking maybe Missy was wrong, maybe there was time to get help. My stomach tightened up. I was expecting to find Mama beaten and unconscious, figuring it must've been Lester. But she was in her bed, her hands crossed on her chest, the covers up to her armpits. There was an empty prescription bottle beside her. She was stiff. I didn't have to touch her to know it was too late.

She looked surprised. Maybe dying hadn't felt like she thought it would. Her auburn hair was brushed all nice and she had a tiny bit of makeup on, like when she was going out. She'd put on perfume, too, but I could still smell death.

I looked away.

Her interview suit was draped across the chair, an envelope with my name on it leaning against it. She must have been getting ready to go look for work again when it all caught up with her.

"You better read that before the police get in here and take it," said Shenia.

She was standing right behind me, holding Missy's hand. I hadn't even realized Shenia had followed me—but of course she had, I'd taken off with her cell phone! I gave it back to her.

She was right about the police. She should know. Her father was a cop. He'd grown up in that house they lived in and he owned it. Otherwise she'd never be in this neighborhood.

I picked up the envelope and tried to open it gently, but the glue was too good. I ended up tearing it. It felt like I was ripping Mama apart. I read the shaky writing to myself. *I can't do anything right.*

I thought of her laughing on the river, back when Swede was alive. She hadn't laughed hardly at all since then.

The last was scribbled. *Stay together.*

She hadn't signed it.

I let the letter drop onto the side of Mama's bed, like it was too heavy to hold.

"There's another envelope." Shenia pointed at the bedside table.

I went and picked it up. I'd seen it last night. It was to my mother's mother. Mama had been so desperate that she'd been ready to beg for help from them. Well, almost ready. It was sealed and stamped, but she hadn't mailed it. I shoved that envelope into my pocket and ignored the questions on Shenia's face.

Mama's life would have been a lot easier without me. She'd be alive and happy.

"What did Mama say?" Missy whispered.

"She said we need to stick together."

She handed me Mama's cell phone and my apartment key.

"The welfare people will be here as soon as we call this in," warned Shenia. "There's no way they're gonna have a place for all three of you. You're too old, Michael. They'll probably throw you into juvie just 'cause they don't have any place better."

"What are we gonna do?" Missy whined.

She stood there scared, looking at me like I had all the answers. We both knew what Shenia said was true. It hadn't taken long in this ghetto neighborhood to see how things worked.

Shenia asked, "Did she have any friends or relatives who could take all of you?"

"Maybe."

"Who?" Missy looked bewildered.

Mama hadn't kept up with friends from the old neighborhood or made any here. Lester hadn't wanted her talking to people. If my daddy had any folks, they hadn't kept in touch with his white widow. Swede had been an orphan.

I guess damaged people attract each other.

"We're gonna go to Mama's parents. See if they'll take you and Jimmy in, and I'll find a place to stay nearby."

"Mama's parents?" Missy looked even more confused.

I was the only one who knew Mama had family, and I'd forgotten until she showed me that letter last night, when I was complaining about her not having a job and my having to walk the kids home every day and never having any money for myself. I didn't tell her I knew it was my fault her parents didn't talk to her. Now she'd decided she'd rather die than ask them for help. I wasn't about to explain that to anyone, especially in front of the girl I liked. So I ignored Missy's question.

"Go put as many clothes as you can into your school bag," I said.

"What about Fred?"

Fred was her stuffed dog.

"Only take what you can carry yourself, and make sure you've got plenty of undies," I added, because that's what Mama would have said.

"I'll carry Fred."

"I'll help her pack," said Shenia.

Missy dragged Shenia to our room. I trailed along behind.

Missy showed Shenia the box where she kept her clothes and they started picking out what to take. It was embarrassing to have Shenia see how we'd been living, all three of us crammed into this tiny space—and our mother lying like that in the other room, leaving her kids to manage on their own.

"How are you going to travel?" Shenia asked as they put Fred on top and closed the pack.

"I'll figure that out while I get Jimmy."

"No!" Missy shouted. "Don't leave us here alone."

I told her there was nothing to be afraid of and she started to argue with me, but Shenia interrupted.

"It's okay, Michael. I'll take her over to my house." She turned to Missy. "We'll wait for the boys there, and you can help me look on the computer for ways to get to your grandparents."

I pulled the envelope out of my pocket. "Here's the address. Can you try to find a phone number, too?"

"Sure." Shenia took the envelope and looked at Missy. "Let's go."

Shenia put the pack down and dug deep in her pocket for her keys.

"Missy, honey, can you let go of my hand a minute?"

Missy let go, but she squeezed between Shenia and the door while Shenia stretched her fingers, twisted her grandmother's ring and shifted it a little towards the middle knuckle. Missy's grip hadn't made the ring cut skin, but it hurt. As soon as Shenia opened the door, Missy slipped inside ahead of her. Shenia moved the pack inside and closed the door. She started past the little girl towards the dining room.

"The computer's this way." Shenia heard a click and turned.

Missy had locked the deadbolt.

Shenia's father was always after her to lock up as soon as she got home, since the neighborhood had gone downhill so bad. Probably Missy's mother had told her to do the same thing. Besides, finding her mother that way had to have been scary.

Shenia went back and gave the little girl a hug. "The boys will be here soon. We need to be ready with directions."

"Can I look at the envelope?" Missy asked.

"Sure, honey."

As the computer booted up, Missy examined the address, her face scrunched together.

Then she sighed and handed it to Shenia. "I can't read cursive."

"Mrs. Michael Dolan, North East, Pennsylvania." Shenia looked again and cried out, "Pennsylvania! That's all the way across the country."

She'd never see Michael again.

"For real?" asked Missy. "Mama's parents live in Pennsylvania?"

"Yeah, that's what it says."

"That's way far away from here?"

Shenia nodded.

"Good." The little girl seemed to relax a little.

With the memories she had from today, that made sense.

Shenia tried to put her own feelings aside. She just hoped Missy wouldn't be disappointed by the grandparents she'd never even known about.

"Watch me do a people search for your grandpa. Maybe we can find a phone number."

The number came up right away.

"Let's call him," said Missy.

"No, we'll wait for Michael."

Shenia was searching ways to get to Pennsylvania when Missy's stomach growled.

"Let's get you a snack," she told the little girl.

Jimmy was on the ball, racing ahead of everyone else. He never paused as he dribbled in close and kicked it right past the goalie. Soccer was the perfect sport for him. Good thing it was practice. It would have been a lot harder to get him away from a game.

I went up to the coach.

"Our mama sent me to get Jimmy. She needs him at home."

"Is there a problem? He'll still play against Ridgeview tomorrow, won't he?"

I wasn't happy about lying to the man, but it had to be done.

I shook my head. "Mama's got a job interview out of town and she's taking us with her. I don't think we'll be back for the game."

The coach called Jimmy in from the field. The kid grabbed his stuff and headed down the street with me right away, mad as he could be after the coach told him why I was there.

"They need me to beat Ridgeview. Why's Mama got to take us along?"

"She can't leave us home alone."

"Why not? You'd be with us. Besides, Mama's supposed to cut my hair tonight."

Mama had buzzed him before school started. It was November now and he was starting to look like a girl. The bangs probably got in his way on the field, too.

I couldn't tell him out there on the street, but I couldn't let him stay angry, either. "Don't be mad at Mama. It's not her fault."

"What do you mean?"

I didn't answer. I stretched my legs out and walked so fast he had to trot to keep up. That kept him quiet until we got to the apartment. Once we were inside, I told him. I couldn't think of a way to say it gently, so I did it quick.

"Mama's gone, Jimmy. She's up in her bed. She killed herself."

"No!" he cried. He ran to see for himself, like I'd known he would.

I followed up the stairs with feet full of lead. He was standing there by the bed, the tears pouring down his face.

"Why'd she do it? Why'd she leave us?"

I had the same questions and no good answers, but I tried. "You know how worried she was, how she's felt she wasn't taking good care of us."

"But now she can't take care of us at all. What are we gonna do?"

Already the pressure was getting to me, but I just had to deal with it. I was all the kids had left. It was on me to keep them together. That's what Mama's letter said.

"We're gonna get out of here before anyone finds out and splits us up. Shenia will call the police tomorrow."

I hadn't asked her yet, but I knew she would. "That'll give us a head start."

"Where'll we go?"

"I've got the address for Mama's parents." Then I had to explain to Jimmy that yes, Mama had parents we'd never seen.

"Missy's over at Shenia's house ready to go. We need to pack up our stuff."

We went to our room and dumped our school stuff on the bed.

Jimmy had a small duffel bag. The first thing he did was put his soccer ball back into it.

"You can't take that," I told him. "You have to get all your clothes in there."

He ignored me and started shoving underwear around the ball.

"Jimmy, you have to listen to me now."

"Mama gave it to me." He pushed deeper. "I'll make it all fit. I don't need many clothes."

He was still blinking back tears and snuffling. I quit arguing with him.

When we were done, he asked, "Will the police come after us?"

"Maybe. But in a city this big, maybe they'll be too busy."

I didn't really believe that, but I was hoping.

"We should get all our pictures out of the house, to slow them down," he said.

I hadn't thought of that. I found an empty box in the hall closet and we took photos off the walls and table tops, upstairs and down. We could leave them with Shenia for now.

"Where do our grandparents live?" Jimmy asked.

"Pennsylvania."

"Won't it cost a lot of money to get there?"

I nodded. I hadn't thought about that, either. Then I saw Mama's purse on a table by the couch. Jimmy saw me looking at it. He picked it up and handed it to me. Reluctantly, I pulled out her wallet. There was a picture of all of us, but she didn't have a single dollar in there. I took the photo and all of her cards, stuck them into my left cargo pocket, and then buttoned it shut.

"You know which house is Shenia's, don't you?"

"Yeah."

"You head on over. I'll be there in a minute."

"I'll wait for you."

"No."

Today had been warm and sunny, but there'd been some cold days last week, so the kids' jackets were on hooks near the door. I handed them to Jimmy.

"Take these. We'll need them. I'm going to get my heavy hoody and I'll be right behind you."

With his arms full, he didn't want to stand around. I watched him cross the street and walk up to Shenia's door, then I went back inside our apartment.

I dragged myself up the stairs to Mama's room.

Alone with what was left of her, the sorrow welled up in my chest and pushed tears down my face. For a while, I let them flow. Finally I started to blink, trying to stop them, but it felt like someone was squeezing them right out of my heart.

"Why'd you give up?" My voice ripped the air.

The sound of it shoved me into action. I put her suicide note on the chair where we'd found it. I crumpled the ruined envelope and threw it into her wastebasket. I stared at the note, then glared at her.

"It isn't fair," I gasped. I kept sucking in air, trying not to cry anymore, 'til my head started getting light and my legs went so wombly I sat down on the floor right where I was.

Hyperventilation. Swede had told me not to do that to swim underwater farther, that I could pass out. I couldn't afford that now. I was scared, but the kids needed me to be strong. I made myself hold the air inside until the oxygen could get to my blood, then exhaled slowly. After a few more slow, deep breaths to steady myself, I stood up and took my last look at Mama.

"You better be watching over us."

I got the hoody, glanced around our room, then got out of there as quick as I could. As my key turned the deadbolt in the front door, my stomach cramped. I hated leaving Mama's body alone in the apartment like that, but it had to be done.

Shenia met me outside her house. "You realize your grandparents live across the country?"

"Yeah, I saw that last night when Mama showed me the letter."

"You don't even know them, do you?"

She asked so softly I couldn't lie. I couldn't talk, so I just shook my head. It felt like she was looking right through me.

"I found a phone number for your grandfather, but maybe it would be better if you were away from here before you call."

"That's what I was thinking." I figured it would be harder to say no if we were on our way. And if they did say no, I'd have a better chance to figure something out before anyone caught up to us.

"I know it sounds awful, but it would be better if your mother wasn't found too soon," Shenia said.

"I know. I was going to ask you to call the police tomorrow."

"I'll wait until you call to let me know you're okay."

"Good. You better not admit you were there today, though."

She shrugged one shoulder. "I'll tell them you called me. That'll be true. There's no one else with a key?"

"Just me. She meant for me to find her."

"You didn't know that when you let Missy go ahead... Isn't there an apartment manager or someone who has one?"

"He might, but he stays away unless we call with a complaint. And I'm not sure she gave him the new key yet. We changed the locks after Lester moved out."

"Has he been bothering her?" asked Shenia.

I wished I could say yes. That he'd come back and hurt Mama had been my first thought today. I'd like for it to be his fault Mama killed herself. But the truth was, I hadn't seen him since he left last July, and I was the one who'd made Mama feel worse last night. I shook my head.

"Good." Shenia paused a moment, then said, "I didn't miss what you told Missy, that your grandparents might take her and Jimmy, but not you. It's a color thing, isn't it?"

My throat had a big knot stuck in it. I couldn't look at her.

She put a hand on my arm. "Well, if they take the little ones in and there's nowhere for you to go, you come back here and we'll find a place."

I cracked a smile and croaked, "Thanks."

Sure felt good to be wanted. Then she gave me a hug and a quick kiss right on the lips. Before I could move, she opened the door and was gone inside the house.

The shock went right through me like electricity. Even that little peck. I'd been thinking of what it would be like to kiss her for months. But guilt was on me even as she opened the door. My mama was lying cold in her bed. Shenia just meant it to be friendly, to try and make me feel better. I followed her inside.

Not only had she started looking stuff up on the internet, she also had a frozen pizza in the oven and the kids sitting in front of the TV. I don't think either of them really knew what they were watching, but it was helping them wait quietly. Shenia took me to where her laptop was set up. Just a few doors away from us and she had a completely different life. She was flipping from one screen to another when a buzzer went off in the kitchen.

"That's the pizza. You want to check out the buses and trains?"

We'd never had a computer or a smart phone. I avoided them at school so no one would know how little I knew. Kept telling myself I'd get to it someday, but the distance between me and those machines seemed to get wider all the time. Now Shenia would think I was stupid, but we couldn't afford to waste time with me faking it.

"I'll get the pizza," I said. "I'm not that good on computers."

"Okay." She didn't seem to care. "Plates are in the cupboard to the right of the sink. There's soda in the fridge and glasses on the shelf above the plates."

I headed for the kitchen. The pizza was done. There was an oven mitt hanging on a little hook by the stove. I wasn't sure I should use it, 'cause it matched the towels that were folded neatly over a rack by the sink. Nothing was stained.

I'd never been in Shenia's house before, but it suited her mother, from what I'd seen of the lady.

The pizza would burn if I didn't get it out, so I used the fancy mitt, being careful not to get any sauce on it, then I put it back on its hook. The plates and glasses were right where she'd said, but it took some looking to find something to cut the pizza. I could have asked, but I wanted to show Shenia I wasn't completely useless. I set it up to eat in the kitchen, then went to get the kids. Missy was leaning against Jimmy.

"We better eat," I told them.

Missy trailed after Jimmy, hanging onto his shirttail. Well, she'd found Mama. I guessed she was entitled to be kinda clingy for a while. I stopped by Shenia.

"You done yet?" I asked. "Pizza's ready."

"No, not quite. You go ahead. I'm not hungry."

"You sure?" I was letting her do all the work.

"Jimmy said you've got your mother's credit cards?"

"Here's everything that was in her wallet."

Shenia took all of it. "I'll check the balances while you eat."

"You can do that?"

"The recordings will give all that information. You know her social security number and date of birth if they ask?"

"I know her birthday, but she wouldn't tell us her age."

She shuffled through Mama's cards. "Here's her license and social security card. Lynn Johnson. You're lucky, that can be a guy's name. You can use her credit cards, easy."

"Unless they ask for ID."

"Most places don't. I use my mother's card all the time." At the look on my face, she added, "Only when she says I can. They never ask for ID. What's her mother's maiden name? Sometimes they ask for that when you call the credit card company."

I only knew because I'd needed it for a school project.

"Angelina DeNiro."

"Like the actor?"

"Yeah. No relation." But it had been easy to remember. And I'd wondered how anyone named Angelina could cut off her own daughter, even if she hated the daughter's husband and child.

Shenia was still clicking away on the computer, so I joined the kids in the kitchen. The pizza went down like cardboard, but we had to eat. I forced my way through two pieces, then left them picking at theirs and went back to Shenia.

"We've got a problem," she said.

The pizza pushed up against the top of my stomach. "What?"

"Your bus left half an hour ago, at 3:52. The next one's not until 3:35 in the morning. You want to wait around for the bus that long, downtown with the kids, in the middle of the night?"

"What about the train?"

"The train would have been easier—you're going to change buses a few times—but Amtrak's real strict on traveling with kids. You'd need phony ID saying you were eighteen, and we don't have time for that. The bus lets a fifteen-year-old travel with kids."

"But the bus already left."

"Give me a minute."

She had the schedule on the screen. She clicked the corner and that screen disappeared and she pulled up a new one.

"What are you doing?" I asked.

"Figuring out if you can catch the bus in Reno. It stays there almost an hour... Yes! It takes just over two hours to drive to Reno. It's almost 4:30 now, so you have three hours to get there and get your tickets." She clicked to print something.

"And how do we get to Reno?"

"Your mother's car. It works, right?"

I felt the blood rush to my face. All that was happening and I could still be embarrassed to admit I couldn't drive yet.

"I'm fifteen, Shenia. I don't have a permit yet."

"Well, I'm sixteen, and I have my license."

"I haven't seen you driving."

"My parents usually have their cars."

"Can you drive a stick shift?"

"My ex-boyfriend showed me how on his car."

"What would your daddy say if he knew you drove us to Reno?"

She layered on the ghetto sound as she said, "What he don't know, don't hurt him."

I wasn't convinced, but there wasn't much choice. I'd never driven in traffic and rush hour wasn't the time to start, especially how I was feeling. And if we didn't get far away before they found Mama, we'd be split up for sure. We had to get to her parents. They'd take in both their cute little white grandkids. At least the two of them would be together. I could probably find a way to stay nearby.

"Did you call the credit cards?" I asked.

"There's only one good one; the others are maxed out. This one's got enough to pay for your bus tickets, gas to get to Reno, and still leave some for meals on the trip."

"Are you sure you want to drive us all the way to Reno?"

Shenia crossed her arms. "What kind of friend would I be if I didn't?"

My heart swelled up and tears threatened to start flowing again. "Thanks," was all I could say.

"I'll grab a few things and be ready to go in a minute. Do you have the car keys? I don't know how to do that hot-wire shit." She was trying to lighten it up for me.

"They're probably in her purse."

"Guess you'll have to go get them. Where's the car?"

"In the lot behind the building. But what if someone sees us? Sees you driving us off in Mama's car?"

"As long as you act like you're supposed to be doing whatever you're doing, nobody pays any attention." Shenia sounded kind of impatient.

"We cleaned up the kitchen," said Jimmy.

He was standing in the doorway, holding Missy's hand. They both had clean faces, too.

"You and Missy take your stuff to Mama's car. Shenia's going to drive us to catch the bus. I'll get the keys and meet you there."

"Can we wait for Shenia?" asked Missy. She was way quieter than her usual self.

"Sure, honey," said Shenia.

I headed to the apartment for Mama's car keys.

-8-

Walking back there, all I could think of was Mama, dying all alone in that bed upstairs, and how our last words were angry.

Normally, first thing I do after school is go for the jug of milk in the fridge. But there wasn't any yesterday. I complained to Mama and one thing led to another, and we started shouting and she was crying at the same time, saying she was trying everything she knew how to do. She waved that letter at me and said how she was even begging for help from her parents, who'd cut her off after she married my father.

Then she shut herself in her room. I could hear her crying, and I knew how desperate she must be feeling to write to them, and I knew it was really me they'd rejected, not her.

But I didn't try to make her feel better.

The key didn't want to go into the lock. I finally figured out I had it upside down. Inside, I went straight for her purse and searched through it. No keys. My pack suddenly felt too heavy to carry. I slid it off, then dumped Mama's purse out on the couch and checked every little pocket. But I still didn't find anything. I even put each thing back one at a time, thinking maybe I was looking right at the keys and not seeing them. But they were not in her purse.

The stairs were there staring at me. Instead I went to the kitchen. Sometimes she left her keys on the shelf when she came in the back door. I hadn't even gone into the kitchen this afternoon. I'd gone straight upstairs. There was a grocery bag on the shelf and a brand new jug of milk sitting there, going bad. The depression must have hit her hard and fast. I clenched my jaw and looked for the keys. They weren't on the counter, but the phone charger was. I stuck it in my pocket with the phone. She must have carried the keys upstairs.

I didn't want to go back up there. It felt like the whole place, the whole day, was pressing down on me. And the milk was sitting there, starting to sour.

"Dammit!" I screamed, and I slammed it across the room.

It exploded against the cupboards and milk sprayed all over half the floor. Then I saw the drawer next to the refrigerator. I tried not to step in the milk as I crossed over to it. The extra car key was there. I could breathe again.

I wouldn't have to go back up to her room.

I slipped the spare onto my key ring so it wouldn't get lost, then grabbed a bag of tortilla chips and got a two-liter of cola out of the fridge. Eventually we'd be hungry and there might not be anyplace to buy food with the credit card right when we wanted it.

I double-checked Mama's hidey-place for cash—the casserole dish in the corner cupboard—but there was nothing there. She used to keep at least a hundred in the house all the time. She must've been using credit cards for everything. We were lucky there was one left she hadn't maxed out.

I went back to the living room for my pack and double-checked that I'd locked up the front good. This time I thought to make sure all of the downstairs windows were latched shut. On my way out I made sure to lock the back door too, handle and deadbolt.

Unless the super had a key, no one was going to get in there.

-9-

When Michael exploded in the kitchen, Shenia had just closed the back of the Explorer. She checked, but the kids were in the back seat getting settled and didn't seem to have heard. The curtain on the neighbor's window moved a bit, though. Shenia tilted her face away from view as she got into the driver's seat.

She didn't want him to freak, but she'd brought a bag of her own clothes as well as her jacket and laptop, as well as the debit card her mother kept at the house for emergencies. It wasn't that she planned to go on with them, not really. But if Michael asked her to come along to help with Missy, well, it would be nice to have a few more days. If they had that time together, there was a better chance a long-distance relationship might work.

She moved the seat back a notch and adjusted the mirrors.

"You kids have your seatbelts on?"

She was answered by two clicks and mumbled affirmatives. She glanced back at the kids. Missy was staring out the window away from the apartments, her little body stiff with stress. Poor thing, finding her mother like that. Shenia had been a teenager when her grandmother passed, and it had still been hard.

Missy might need some counseling to get through this. Hopefully her grandparents would see to that. Meanwhile, the best thing was to keep her thinking about other things.

"I'm going to drive all of you to Reno to catch the bus."

"Reno? That's way far," said Jimmy.

"The bus already left here, but they make so many stops and stay there so long, we'll be able to get you onto it. Then it'll be an easy trip to your grandparents."

"Mama never even talked about them," said Jimmy.

Missy turned away from the window. "They're real far away. That's good."

"Yeah, I guess," said Jimmy, but his voice was laden with doubt.

"Sure it'll be good," Shenia said cheerfully. "It's hard to keep up with family when there's a whole country between."

"We'll be safe there," said Missy.

-10-

Mama hadn't even locked the car. The kids and Shenia were sitting in it, ready to go. I opened the back of Swede's old Explorer and put my pack and the snacks in with everything else. Shenia had her pack and a coat and her laptop in there. I shut the hatch and got into the passenger seat.

"Why'd you bring so much stuff?" I asked.

"You never know. The kids have their warm jackets, do you?"

"Outgrew mine. I've been wearing my hoody."

"Well, maybe that'll be enough riding the bus."

It was nice, her worrying about me that way. "Why'd you bring your computer?"

"If we need more directions or anything, we can find a Wi-Fi hotspot. If I had my smart phone, all I'd need is a signal, but my parents got annoyed with how much data I was using and gave me that antique."

So that's why she had a flip phone like Mama's. But she wasn't a techno idiot like me. We'd never had a smart phone or a computer. When we used them in school, I goofed off so no one would see how stupid I was. I'd always wondered why everyone could use their phones for internet anywhere, but if I asked her about it now, I'd look dumb to the girl I wanted to impress.

She reached out for the car keys. Our hands touched as I gave them to her. My body remembered how that kiss had felt. At least I didn't gasp out loud.

"I saw you have emergency supplies back there," she said.

"Yeah, Swede taught me to keep a blanket, toolkit, flashlight, a quart of oil and a jug of distilled water in the car at all times. He was worried about leaving us such an old vehicle, but there wasn't money for a newer one."

Shenia knew all about Swede and how much I missed him. She pulled an MP3 player out of her pocket.

"At least they let me keep this."

I heard a seatbelt open and turned to check on the kids. Jimmy was hanging over the back seat, getting the blanket.

"In case we need it later," he explained.

"You don't have an MP3 jack?" Shenia had given up finding it.

"No."

"What is that thing? A cassette player?"

"It doesn't work. All we've got is the radio."

She stared at me a moment, then handed her MP3 player to Jimmy. "Put this in my pack, would you?" She turned to me. "Think you can find some music on that thing?"

It was set to Mama's favorite oldies station. Shenia shook her head and sighed, then started the car. I changed it to KSFM.

"That's more like it," she said. "Your seat belt on again, Jimmy?"

"Yep."

She started to back up. The car stalled with a jerk.

"Don't worry about that, I just have to get used to a different clutch, that's all," she said.

I didn't want to make her nervous, so I kept my mouth shut.

"Can you read a map?" she asked, handing me three sheets of paper she'd had tucked beside her seat.

"Yeah," I answered, kind of offended.

"Help me get to the freeway."

"I don't need a map for that."

"Good. Just tell me where to turn. Ahead of time."

Shenia didn't drive fast, but she slammed on the brakes for every stop sign or red light, then jerked and burned rubber half the time when she started back up. It was a miracle we didn't get stopped. The kids stayed really quiet.

When I glanced back, Jimmy widened his eyes and looked over at Shenia, as if to ask if she knew what she was doing. I dropped my left hand back between the seats and crossed my fingers. He tightened his seat belt. Missy was looking out the back window, probably missing Mama, not paying any attention to us.

Finally, we were a block from the interstate that would take us all the way to Reno.

"You're gonna need the right lane," I warned her one traffic light ahead of time.

She managed to get over without any trouble because it was still rush hour, so traffic was slower than normal. But in Sacramento, that didn't mean it was crawling, especially on the freeway. As we headed up the ramp, Shenia was gripping that steering wheel hard enough to strangle it, but she merged into the eastbound traffic without a hitch.

At first she stayed in the right lane, but every time she left enough space ahead of us in case she had to stop, people cut through it to get on or off the freeway. She ended up having to change gears up and down so much that she eased over to the next lane instead. It wasn't much better, so when the carpool lane started, she moved over to it one lane at a time.

"Make sure you sit up tall enough to be seen, kids," she said. "I'm not sure if it's two or three we have to have for this lane, and I sure don't want to get stopped."

There weren't as many cars cutting in and out of the express lane, and only from one side, but she had to drive faster than she was supposed to, to stay with the flow of traffic. She was stiff the first half hour we were on the freeway, and I didn't have to tell the kids to be quiet for her. But she did good and it finally thinned out so she could relax some. So we could *all* relax some.

Traffic slowed down as we started the climb into the Sierras and she moved over into the right lane. Without the city lights, it was full dark out, so it was less likely someone would notice and wonder about a black girl driving a couple little white kids and me.

"How's the gas?" I asked.

"It's between three-quarters and full."

"How far is it to Reno?"

"About 130 miles."

I knew we could go more than twice that far on a tank of gas. Swede had taught me to keep track of the mileage, 'cause if there's a sudden drop, that's telling you the car's got a problem.

"We won't have to stop, but we better fill up in Reno so you'll make it back home for sure," I said.

"How are you kids doing?" Shenia asked.

They didn't answer. I turned to look. They were both sound asleep. That was good. Mama always said that sleep heals.

"Did you bring the phone number for Mama's parents?" I asked.

It would be nice to have privacy when I called, but I knew it was three hours later back there, past eight thirty. That was getting late to call old people, especially when they probably didn't want to hear from you, and with bad news, too.

"It's on the back of the Reno map," Shenia said.

I found it, then pulled out Mama's cell phone.

"Do you know what you're going to say?" Shenia asked.

"I'm not sure."

"You probably don't want to start by telling them their daughter's gone. Even if they weren't on good terms, that'd be harsh."

The longer we kept talking, the less I wanted to call. So I just dialed and pushed send. It seemed to ring forever. They weren't home. When I heard the recorded voice, I thought for sure I'd gotten a wrong number, except it had to be right.

Stunned, I hung up.

"Wrong number?" asked Shenia.

"No," I said, hitting redial. I put it on speaker phone this time.

The message said, "The only person who should be callin' this number is Ms. Lynn Marie Dolan McCarthy, and/or her child. If that ain't you, hang up and don't you call this number again. If it is, well then halleluiah, praise the Lord, leave a message with your phone number."

Shenia said what I was thinking. "That woman is black!"

This time, I left my name and Mama's cell phone number.

-11-

"That woman is black," Shenia repeated. "African American woman of color black like me. That doesn't make sense, does it?"

"No. It doesn't make sense at all."

"Maybe she's a maid or a nurse or something. But why would they have her leave the message?"

"And scare away any other callers," I added.

"That's weird, too. You sure you want to take the kids to these people?"

"There's no one else, Shenia. If I dropped out of school and lied about my age to get work, we'd still always be hiding from social services. And the kids would be bringing themselves up 'cause it would probably take me two, three jobs to take care of them."

"Well, maybe they'll call you back before you get there. You can see how they sound direct before you let them near the kids."

"Yeah, I hope so."

I'd looked at the bus schedule Shenia had printed out. This was Wednesday. We wouldn't get to Erie until Saturday morning. She'd printed a map of how to get from there to North East, 'cause it didn't look like the bus stopped in that little town.

It would be nice to know someone would be waiting for us at the station to take us the last part of the way. At least that message sounded like they wanted to hear from us. I'd hang onto that.

We drove up into the mountains in silence, except for the radio and a light snore from Jimmy once in a while. Shenia was a lot more relaxed now there were hardly any other cars on the road, but she was still a new driver, and I didn't want to distract her.

The car ran fine climbing all the way to the summit at Donner Pass. When we crossed into Nevada, I took a look at the map that showed how to get to the bus station.

"It's Exit 12, Keystone," I told Shenia.

It still mostly dark at Exit 8, but finally there were signs for fast food and gas, then more houses and billboards for shows, and Home Depot. Then we came around a curve and there were all the casino buildings up ahead, bright and gaudy, and our exit, too.

"It's the business loop," Shenia read. "What do I do now?"

"Turn right, then left on Fourth." It was only a few blocks. We passed McDonald's and Jack in the Box and my stomach grumbled. Then I noticed a Chevron and a Texaco. "It's not even seven. Pull in and get some gas and I'll check the oil before you head home."

"I want to make sure we've found the bus station." She turned left onto Fourth. "What's the next turn?"

"Stevenson, then we're there."

I was going to argue we should get gas first, but then I saw it, lit up and high in the air: Walton Funeral Home Parking Plaza.

A parking plaza for a funeral home. Funerals that would need a whole plaza for parking. I'd been to two funerals and neither one had many people at it. Now Mama wouldn't even have us. I wanted to ask Shenia if she knew what they'd do with Mama, but I couldn't.

Then we passed the funeral home itself, but no, it was a different one, with another big bright sign lighting up the night as if they wanted to make sure the dead didn't miss their stop. I'd never been to a funeral at night. The signs had to be for the dead. Then came a house with a palm reader's neon sign in the window. She was in the right neighborhood for talking to spirits.

"There's a bus!"

Shenia's voice brought me back out of myself. She turned right on Stevenson as if she'd been there before.

I still wondered what they'd do with Mama, though.

"Good thing I saw that bus out behind the building," she said. "That tree covers up the sign some."

There were a few people on the street outside of the bus depot and I turned to wake up the kids, but Shenia's shout had already done that. She drove past and turned right at the next corner.

"I'll head back to one of those gas stations, now I know you have plenty of time to get your tickets," she said.

"Where are we?" asked Jimmy.

"Reno," I said. "The bus won't leave for about forty minutes."

When we got back to Keystone, there was a station, City Corner Gas & Grocery.

"Pull in there," I said. "The name stations probably cost more."

"I need to pee," said Missy.

"I'll take you," said Jimmy.

"Watch outside the door and bring her back here before you go yourself," Shenia warned. She dug her pack out of the back and got her cell phone out. "I'm going to call the local bus station and make sure they won't give you a hard time. I put the Reno number in my phone when I printed the directions."

Soon she was chatting woman-to-woman with the ticket lady.

I listened while I pumped the gas.

"Ruby, do you mind if I call you Ruby?"

Shenia was talking in proper English, like she would at school, only she'd dropped her voice some to sound older. It was kind of husky, and sexy.

"My children are going to be there soon to catch the bus to Erie, Pennsylvania. My older boy's in high school. He'll be with his little brother and sister."

She paused long enough for Ruby to say uh-huh or something, then continued, "Oh, he's a big boy, very mature for his age. I have complete confidence in him. I'm only calling because I can't bring them down there myself. I have to catch a plane to L.A. for a gig—it's a last minute deal, they had someone else and she cancelled—and I wanted to make sure they won't have any problems getting their tickets and getting on the bus. I'll be out of town for a month, so they have to go back to stay with my parents, it's absolutely the only way, and I'm not getting paid enough to buy all three of them plane tickets at the last minute."

Ruby must have talked some then, long enough for Jimmy to bring Missy back to the car and go inside by himself.

Shenia started talking on the phone again. "Michael will have my credit card for the tickets, unless you'd rather I did that now?"

Ruby must have said she'd take the card from me, because Shenia thanked her effusively. I finished pumping gas as she ended the call.

"So our mama's a movie star?" I grinned.

"Or a musician, or somethin' like that, honey. Someone flakey 'nough to send ya'll 'cross country by yo' selves."

Shenia's exaggerated drawl made Missy laugh. That was a good sound. Maybe she'd be okay after all.

In her normal voice, Shenia told me, "Remember, your last name's Johnson for this trip, same as the kids and your Mama's credit cards."

"Not a problem. I went by Johnson most of grade school."

Actually, I'd always been registered as Michael McCarthy. But after Mama had Jimmy and started using Swede's name, I started putting Johnson on everything and the grade school teachers let it slide. But seventh grade on they made me use my official name. I'd finally gotten used to it, but Johnson would still be comfortable.

Shenia was pushing buttons on her cell phone.

"My daddy's called four times."

"Is he always like that? It's not even late."

"No, but I didn't leave a note where I was going, either. He said he was working tonight, filling in for somebody. Thought I'd be home long before him."

"What about your mama?" I asked.

"Mother's visiting my Auntie Char in San Francisco this week. Christmas shopping."

"It's the beginning of November."

"She likes to get it done before the crowds."

While she called her voicemail, I checked the oil. Mama had been having to add some now and then. I didn't want Shenia to have car problems on the way home and get into more trouble because of us. It was at the edge of the fill line so I put in the emergency quart we kept in the car. When I closed the hood, Shenia was gone. The kids were in the car ready to go.

"Where's Shenia?" I asked.

Jimmy nodded toward the building.

"I need to wash up too. We'll be out in a minute. You two stay in the car, and lock the doors." That's what Mama would have told them to do, especially in a city like this.

-12-

The battered Toyota backed into a parking space at the end of Stevenson Street. He turned off his lights. In the dark, no one would notice him as he watched the bus station.

She had to have dropped them off. The Explorer was gone, but why else would she have driven down this one block street? The bus station took up one entire side and the other was a parking lot. He'd wait and see which bus they took.

They had to be running from him.

It wouldn't work.

-13-

Shenia leaned against the restroom wall and listened to the messages from her father one more time.

"Shenia, honey, where are you? I had a call in the neighborhood and stopped at the house. You didn't leave a note."

He used his guilt trip voice for that message.

The next time he sounded concerned.

"Do you know where that boy is? The one you like so much? I need to talk to him as soon as possible."

Then an hour later he'd called again, angry.

"Shenia, you were seen driving away with those kids. Call me."

The last call came a few minutes later. He sounded frightened.

"The neighbor heard him shouting at his mother last night. Now she's dead. Please baby, get away from him."

There was a soft tap.

"You okay?" Michael asked through the door.

"I'll be a minute. Wait for me out in the car."

She stood staring at her phone.

Her father didn't think Michael's mother had committed suicide. What hadn't they seen?

She wanted to call and find out, but she didn't dare. He seemed to be blaming Michael. Why would he do that? It didn't matter. If she called, he'd find them and Michael would be in trouble and he might never see the kids again. She couldn't let that happen.

She put her phone on silent. On the way to the car, she tossed it into the back of a pickup with California plates.

Wednesday Evening: Change of Plans

-14-

"What did you do that for?" Shenia had thrown her phone into the back of that truck—was she nuts?

She got into the car and just sat there.

"We'll miss the bus," I said. "What's wrong?"

She stared at me without answering.

I was about to burst when finally she spoke.

"You can't buy bus tickets with that credit card and I can't go home."

"What?"

"We've got to drive to your grandparents, and we better get to an ATM and get as much cash as we can right now, before they track down your mother's credit cards."

"Why? What'd your daddy say?"

"They found your mother."

"How?"

"I don't know."

"Good," said Jimmy. "They'll take care of her."

"I'm glad, too, Jimmy, but they may try to stop us," I said. "Are they already looking for us?"

"Or will be soon," said Shenia.

"So they'll track Mama's credit card."

Shenia nodded. "Good thing we hadn't bought those tickets yet."

"Okay," I said. "I get why we can't use the credit card for tickets, they'd know where we were going and how. But that doesn't mean you can't go home. We'll find another way to get there."

"Your neighbor saw us leave. My daddy knows I've been talking to a boy over at the apartments, so he figured out it was me driving."

"It could have been some other girl. You could park the car up at the elementary school and walk home. You could act like you had no idea what was going on."

Shenia shook her head. "You haven't met my daddy. Once he knows I'm up to something, he doesn't let go. He'd have me telling the whole truth and nothing but the truth in two minutes flat. Besides, you need me to drive. How else would you get there?"

"Maybe we should go back," said Jimmy.

"No!" Missy wailed. "We can't go back!"

"Don't worry, honey," said Shenia. "We'll take you to your grandparents."

"You're sure?" I asked.

"I'm sure. You better get rid of your phone, too," said Shenia. "Let them track that truck. But turn off the ringer so he won't hear if anyone tries to reach us."

The guy with the truck was staring at the numbers turning on his pump. I tossed Mama's phone in with Shenia's.

"The clerk gave me directions to a Super Walmart," Shenia said. "We'll load up on supplies there, and cash from the ATM, then ditch the credit card. How much do you have on you now?"

"None," I admitted, ashamed.

"Not even change?"

I shook my head. She'd agreed to go walking with me Saturday. I wouldn't even have been able to buy her a coffee or anything. But Shenia knew I did odd jobs for people.

"I've been giving everything I make to Mama, to help with the bills," I explained.

"You kids have any cash?" Shenia asked.

"I've got a dollar thirty-five," said Jimmy. "I cleaned out around the machines."

"What?" Shenia exclaimed.

"They let me check under the gambling machines while Missy was in the bathroom. I just had to hurry 'cause I'm not allowed to gamble."

"You did wash good?" demanded Shenia.

"Yes, I washed with soap."

"It's okay. Jimmy always checks machines," I told her. "Mama used to say she didn't have to worry about him starving if he ever got lost."

"My mother would kill me if I'd ever done that."

I had to defend Mama. "Ours wanted us to be ourselves."

"Whatever," snapped Shenia.

She pulled out of the station and turned left. In a few blocks it was obvious we were heading out of town. There were empty railroad tracks on the left, and vacant stores on the right. Then the four-lane divided highway narrowed down to a little two-lane road.

I didn't want to start arguing again, so I kept my mouth shut.

Finally, Jimmy asked, "Are you sure we're going the right way?"

"There's still a bike lane," Shenia said. "Let's give it a few more minutes."

The speed limit went up to forty-five, then we hit Wildflower, which seemed to be its own village. How were we going to find our way across the country if we were already lost?

-15-

No buses had loaded. What if the kids weren't here? They could be on their way back to Sacramento to talk to the cops.

Another half hour; he'd give it another thirty minutes.

Maybe.

-16-

Shenia had been going the right direction. The Walmart was on the edge of town with a bunch of other big stores.

"Jimmy, Missy, stay together, close but not right next to us," I said. "People would be sure to remember two little blonde kids with a beautiful African American young woman and me."

"You go right ahead and flatter me, Michael McCarthy. You know you turn heads yourself." Shenia smiled.

She thought I was hot! And my flattery had worked—she wasn't mad anymore.

"What's your mother's PIN?" she asked.

"Pin?" I'd never used anything but cash.

"Shoot. Let me see your mother's credit card." Shenia turned it over. "She wrote a code on the back—MDMmd. You'd be MDM. It's probably your birthday, month and day, in four digits."

"Why four digits?"

"PINs are usually four digits."

"Oh." I felt stupid. "That'd be 0806, then."

"We can't look like a couple of kids goofing around at the ATM machine or they'll come check us out," she warned as we entered the store.

"You better stay with me, though. I've never used one."

"Okay. Just don't act the fool."

I didn't know enough to take care of myself, let alone the kids. We got the cash first. I could only get three hundred in one day.

"That won't be enough," said Shenia. She pulled out her mother's debit card.

"We're not going to use your mother's money."

"Only if we need to, but we should get the cash while we can."

She got five hundred more and I put all the money in the cargo pocket with Mama's letter to her mother. It wouldn't get lost there.

"We better buy what we need and get out of here as soon as we can," Shenia said. "Before they call the credit companies. We need blankets so we can sleep in the car and a jacket for you. That and groceries will wipe out what's left on your mother's credit card."

"We only need a couple days' worth of food."

"It'll take longer than the bus if we don't drive during the day, or if we have to get off the interstate," she insisted.

I was sure there was something she wasn't telling me.

We moved fast, up one aisle and down the next, the kids dawdling across the ends so we could keep track of them without seeming to be together.

We skipped the frozen sections, but picked up a cooler and ice so we could get milk and some other cold things. Shenia made sure we got bananas and oranges and granola bars and water. I probably would have gotten mostly junk food. But I was the one who spotted the atlas with maps for the whole country, in case we got off the highway and couldn't find internet.

I thought to grab three quarts of oil, too. That should get us to Pennsylvania. The kids disappeared while I was deciding which brand to get. They came back with a couple coloring books and crayons for Missy and a video game for Jimmy.

"I can't believe this was only a dollar," he said to Missy, for our benefit. He sounded like a commercial for Walmart. He glanced around to make sure no one was watching, then tossed it into the cart. When we went by the electronics, he veered off and got a prepaid phone and brought it back.

"Minutes, too," I said quietly.

At least I knew about prepaid phones. I wasn't a complete techno moron. When we had everything, the kids went to wait by the machines at the front of the store. At the cash register, Shenia signed the receipt Lynn Johnson without batting an eyelash.

She has beautiful eyelashes, too. Thick, and they curl up just enough to make you notice her eyes, but without making her look startled all the time. She has brown eyes flecked with gold.

The cashier looked bored; he didn't ask for ID.

When we were done putting everything into the car, Jimmy asked if we could eat at McDonalds. "None of us ate much pizza."

Shenia hadn't eaten at all. She didn't mention that, but she did say there was probably enough left on Mama's card to pay for it.

"Sit over in the corner," I told the kids.

There weren't any other customers. If any came in, it was better for us to be over out of the way.

"What would you like?" the grey-haired lady asked.

We ordered four combos and an extra double quarter pounder with cheese. Shenia looked at the subtotal.

"Can you add four hot fudge sundaes, to that, but not make them 'til we finish the other food?" she asked.

"Of course," said the lady.

She didn't ask for ID when Shenia ran the credit card through the machine. It took two trays to carry everything to the table.

"One of those burgers for me?" Jimmy asked.

"Sure," said Shenia. "Missy, are you going to eat chicken fingers with me?"

"Okay. But sometime I want to get a Happy Meal." Missy wasn't complaining, not really, it was a habit, something she said every time we went to McDonald's. Mama always said it was too much to pay for a cheap toy. Missy ate the chicken fingers without fussing.

When we were done, Shenia bent the credit card back and forth until it broke and buried it in our trash. I went up for the sundaes while Jimmy finished off the fries.

"Did you and the little ones get enough to eat?" the lady asked.

"Yes, ma'am, thank you." I wasn't happy she was noticing us, but what else did she have to do? I took the sundaes straight back to the table. "Eat these up and let's get out of here," I said quietly.

Everyone dug into their ice cream.

When we were done, Shenia told the kids to use the bathroom there. "Don't know when you'll have another chance. We need to drive as far as we can tonight.

I wanted to ask her what else her father had said, so I hung back and blocked her way while the kids went into the restrooms ahead of us. "Thank you. For everything," I started.

She interrupted, all defensive. "You're not saying goodbye."

"Can't. You're driving."

"You will too, before the end of this trip," she said.

Then she slipped by me into the bathroom.

I'd have to ask her later.

The buses loaded behind the station!

He couldn't be sure which one they'd boarded, if they'd even been here at all. The ticket agents were watching him, probably afraid he might be a terrorist, with the sunglasses and his hood up inside. One of them approached him.

"Can I help you sir?"

He looked at her nametag.

"No, Ruby, I was just checking the schedule. My nephew is coming to visit me next week. The buses unload out back, right?"

"Yes, sir."

"Thank you."

Her cell phone rang as he turned to leave. "My shift's over in five minutes… They didn't show up. That mother must have had an attack of common sense. Really, can you imagine, sending two little children all the way across the country with a teenage boy? And she wasn't even going to see them off. Some people."

That had to be them. He checked the schedule. The only cross-country bus in the last hour went straight across to Pennsylvania. That envelope! She'd said it was for her mother. So that's where they were headed. But why didn't they get on the bus?

Maybe they spotted him. The girl had talked and they were running from him. That was it. They probably thought it would be easier to lose him in the car, but there was only one logical route at this point. He'd catch up to them easily.

Hearsay couldn't hurt him, but the little girl had to go.

-18-

I carried the laptop into a coffee shop that advertised free internet. We left the kids in the car.

"We should really be getting on the road," I said. "That lady at McDonald's noticed us."

"That's why I didn't take the laptop in there," Shenia said.

"We shouldn't have been seen with the kids."

"I suppose we could paint them darker or bleach you lighter, but it all sounds painful." Shenia flashed a smile at me. "You're not gonna turn my chocolate white, that's for sure."

I laughed. Just a little one, then remembered Mama.

Well, maybe she'd be glad. She always loved the sound of laughter. The only time I'd heard hers lately was when I pretended the girl I was talking to on the phone was nobody special. Mama knew better.

I wished I could tell her that Shenia had kissed me.

We sat down and I watched while Shenia checked how to get from Reno to North East, Pennsylvania. She went back and forth between screens a few times, then looked around to make sure nobody was close enough to be listening before she spoke.

"We'll have to use the interstates. It would take way too long otherwise. It's straight to Chicago on eighty, then ninety to North East."

"How long's that take?"

"About thirty-five hours of driving, thirty-eight if we avoid the toll roads where someone might notice us."

"That's faster than the bus. Tonight, all day tomorrow, we'll be there Friday morning!" Finally, something was going right.

"That's without stops. We've been here more than two hours, and I'll need to sleep."

"We'll take turns driving." The words just popped out.

"Thought you didn't know how."

"Swede let me drive off road once; taught me how to handle a skid. That's not the same as driving in traffic, but I can't expect you to drive all the way across the country."

"So you gonna go first?"

"Not here in the city. I'd hit someone for sure."

"We'll wait 'til we're out in the middle of nowhere, then."

"What's the longest you ever stayed up?" I asked.

"About thirty-six hours. But I've been up all day," she said.

"Trading off, we'll get there quick."

Mama's parents would take the kids. Maybe. If not, better to find out sooner than later.

"We might not want to drive during the day." Shenia was staring at the map. "At night there will be less police and other people to notice us."

"You really think we need to worry about the police? What did your daddy say?"

She didn't look at me. "Well, it's your mama's car, so technically we're stealing it."

"They're saying I stole Mama's car?"

"No, I was just thinking, they can use it to find us."

It still felt like she was holding something back, but I had to trust she was right we should travel at night.

"Where will we stay during the day?" I asked.

"Well, we can park at rest stops a couple hours, but I think they get patrolled pretty good." She exhaled hard. "Maybe it *would* be better to keep moving as much as we can."

Now I was really confused. "How hard do you think they're looking for us?"

"I'm not sure."

"With the kids so little, would they put out an Amber Alert?"

"One way to find out," she answered.

She typed "amber alert" in the little white box, then clicked on one of the sites that came up. Someday I'd have to ask her how she picked which one. She went back and tried another, so maybe it was just luck.

"There isn't anything about us here, and the government site says it has to be an abduction with the children at risk of serious harm or death, so I don't think we'll have to deal with that, anyway. But they'll probably put us on NCIC for the car."

"That's for real?" I'd heard it on cop shows.

"Yeah, it's real. It's a computer database. We'll probably be in there as runaways once my daddy shows my picture to your nosey neighbor."

She went back to the map and studied it some more. "Cities are the main place it'll be tricky."

"Jimmy can help watch the signs. It'll keep him busy," I said.

She packed up the computer, then stopped and looked at me. "You remember how to get back to the freeway from here?"

I grinned. "Come on. I'll navigate."

Back in Sacramento, Shenia's father was staring at the box of photos on the floor in her room.

He sighed and picked out what looked like the most recent picture of each of the three children. On his way downstairs, he took Shenia's last school photo off the wall. He set them down long enough to shrug into his uniform coat, even though he was no longer on duty, then he headed across the street.

Yellow tape closed off access to the apartment of the boy that his daughter had apparently helped escape with his younger siblings. He stopped by the patrol car.

"I've got pictures of the kids. Who's on the case?"

"Schuster and Martinez. Schuster was your partner, wasn't he?"

"Yeah."

The cop called the detectives and a few minutes later a balding man in a drab suit came out. He reached for Brown's hand and shook it.

"Sorry to hear your daughter's in the middle of this, Sam."

"I'm glad you're on the case. These are pictures of all the kids. They hid them over at my house."

He knew this made Shenia an accessory after the fact, but he'd learned the hard way not to cover for his children. Besides, the neighbor had been clear that Shenia drove away with them willingly. That already made her culpable. The important thing was to find them, fast.

Schuster hated to let Brown assume the worst, but until they knew more, the older boy was the primary suspect of a probable homicide.

Brown had been the first responder, so he had been first to talk with the neighbor. She'd worried about the kids leaving in the car until finally she went to talk to their mother and found the back door ajar. When she saw the mess in the kitchen and no one answered her shout, she decided to call the police. She hadn't seen anyone visiting the mother for several weeks. The voices she'd heard early that afternoon had been muffled; she'd thought it was the television. But she'd heard Michael arguing with his mother the evening before. That had been loud and clear.

Brown sighed.

Schuster had to offer him something. "You know, the coroner may say it's a suicide."

Brown shook his head. "I saw the marks on her jaw, and the neighbor told me that she was ecstatic about having landed a job finally. Why would she kill herself?"

"Why would the kid kill her?" countered Schuster. "They were arguing about her not having a job."

"He ran. Why would he run if he wasn't guilty?"

-20-

An hour out of Reno we were listening to The River, all music from the sixties and seventies. It was that or Christian or country. When an old Elvis song came on, Shenia snapped it off.

I knew I should make conversation to help her stay alert, but the only thing I could think of was to point out the road signs. "Watch out for deer."

"I saw it. That's why I've got the high beams on."

There wasn't much traffic, so she could leave them on high most of the time. Every bridge we came to had an "icy when wet" sign.

"You think it's cold enough for the bridges to be icy?" I asked.

"It's hard to tell without an outside temperature reading. I wish we had my daddy's car."

She was awfully tense for no traffic. I wondered again what she wasn't telling me, but I couldn't push her about it in front of the kids. Maybe it was just that she wasn't used to driving at night. I wasn't sure if I should talk to her to help her relax or if that would make it harder for her to drive. I decided to stay quiet.

It was spooky out there, as dark as I'd ever seen. Once in a while there'd be a tiny light way off to the side, like someone actually lived out there. It must have been cloudy, too, because there were hardly any stars showing.

Then all of a sudden there were a bunch of tremendously bright lights off to the right, followed by signs warning against emergency stops and forbidding hitchhiking, then a sign for a prison.

And I was responsible for everyone's safety.

We rode along in silence for almost an hour before Shenia asked if I was ready to drive. "We should be almost to the next rest area."

"I guess so."

It came up a few miles later and Shenia pulled off the highway. There were a couple cars parked, but no one we could see. The building area was real dark, with some of the lights not working. A couple of trucks off at the other end sat there rumbling, though.

"Anyone need the restroom?" I asked.

No one wanted to leave the car. I was glad. I'd heard about women meeting truckers at lonely rest areas; I was afraid what the kids might see in this bathroom. Shenia and I got out and switched sides quick. I cracked my knee on the steering column as I got into the driver's seat.

"You could have moved it back," I grumbled.

"Sorry."

I took my time adjusting the seat and the mirrors.

"I can't see anything in these with it dark out," I complained.

"You'll be able to see headlights," she said. "You start with your right foot on the brake and the left on the clutch."

"I know."

"Well, you said you only drove once."

"But I moved it all the time when I was washing it for Mama, back when we had a house and our own driveway."

"Okay. You just let me know when you have a question, then."

"Well, before I start, how do you know how to stay in your lane? Not go over the line, I mean. Or off on the shoulder." I could do it in a driveway, but that was creeping up or back.

"Mostly I look ahead, but you can check by lining up the center of the hood with the right line, if you need to."

I started the car and turned on the lights. I fiddled with them until I knew how to do high and low beams and my turn signals and four-ways.

"You keep doing that and someone will call the cops thinking you're drunk," said Shenia.

The kids giggled. I took a breath, put it into reverse and let my foot off the brake. It started going back with the clutch still on the floor and no gas. I stomped the brake back down, hard.

No one said a word.

I looked over my shoulder good and eased my foot off the brake and coasted. The car curved right back out of that spot like I'd been doing it all my life. Then I put it into first and started away, nice and easy like I'd done in our driveway.

"You've got to get up to speed before you merge onto the highway," said Shenia.

"There's nobody to merge with," I answered.

"Good thing."

Shifting into second, then third, was easier than first. But I couldn't make myself speed up enough to move into fourth. Beyond the edge of the headlights, it was all pitch black.

I tried using the center of the hood like Shenia had said, but I hit a washboard strip they had on the edge of the road and it jerked the wheel. I managed to get back into my lane, but I was driving even slower.

"Just look out far ahead," Shenia said.

Her voice was suspiciously sweet. I figured she was about ready to scream at me, so I tried what she said. It worked a little better. I could see the lines, but outside the headlights it was so dark in every direction that it was like going through a tunnel with a weak flashlight. I was sweating. It seemed like I'd been driving an hour, but I glanced at the clock and it had only been ten minutes. I drifted over onto that strip again.

"You keep driving forty and weaving all over, the first cop that sees us will pull us over for sure," Shenia snapped at me.

"I don't wanna get arrested," whimpered Missy.

"Wouldn't be you, it'd be Michael," Jimmy told her.

"I don't want Michael to go to jail," Missy wailed.

"I'm not going to jail!" I shouted.

Then lights glared off the rearview mirror and blinded me. Someone was coming up fast. He didn't even signal as he swung out to pass us.

It was a triple semi.

I'd seen doubles before, but never a triple. One cab pulling three trailers. I hung on tight to the steering wheel, feeling the truck suck at the Explorer, sure we were going to die, but finally he was ahead and pulling away from us. I tried to speed up then, but never got above forty-five.

No one said a word. When I finally saw an exit sign, I took it—I didn't even have to slow down much for it.

I pulled off onto the shoulder, got out, walked around the car, and opened Shenia's door. I held out the keys.

"You're the one with a license."

She took them without a word and got out of the car. She stretched a little as she walked around to the driver's seat. She pulled it back up where she could reach the pedals. Once she was driving, she seemed to be in a better mood. After we'd been flying through the night for a while, she asked if the kids had nodded off.

I looked back.

"Yeah. I'm amazed Jimmy's out, as much as he slept earlier."

"Well, it's been a hard day. On all of you," she said softly. "Night driving is really tough. You should give it another try tomorrow, when you can see better."

"Thought we were going to rest during the day."

"If you sleep tonight, I can sleep tomorrow."

"While I drive? You're gonna sleep?"

"Once you get the hang of it, I'll probably be able to nod off."

"You gonna be able to stay awake if we're all asleep?"

"If I get too tired, I'll pull over at another rest stop. They're marked on the map and there's plenty of them all along here. And if I have to, I could pull off somewhere like where you did. Only get off on the side road to sleep."

"Don't forget to watch the gas."

"You said we can go three hundred miles?"

"Yeah. But I wouldn't want to push it out in the middle of nothing like this."

She nodded. "I'll look for a gas station once the trip meter says two fifty. Put some cash where I can get it, in case you're asleep when I stop."

I did as she asked, even though I was sure I wouldn't sleep.

-21-

I jerked awake with my heart pounding. "What's wrong?"

"Nothing. I stopped for gas."

I stared at Shenia, confused, then it came to me why she was sitting there in the driver's seat of the Explorer, pushing the trip meter to reset it at zero. Maybe if I went back to sleep, I'd wake up with Mama shaking my arm and telling me to get ready for school.

"The kids didn't wake up at all," Shenia whispered.

I couldn't make it go away; it was real. I stretched my neck side to side and sat up straight as the car slid forward. At least Shenia was here helping.

"You still okay to drive?" My mouth was all cottony.

"Yeah. I got some coffee."

She bumped it as she shifted into second. Ford hadn't adjusted the position of the cup holder for manual transmissions, at least not on this model. I picked up her cup, like I used to do for Mama until she could get into third. Fourth wouldn't bump anything 'cause Shenia hadn't gotten me a drink.

Why would she, though? I'd been asleep while she pumped the gas herself. Once she was on the highway, I put her coffee back and stared out the window.

A few minutes past the gas station and everything was black again, except a few stars. I could have asked her what time it was, but I didn't feel like talking. The clock in the dash said 1:30. Shenia was sitting up straight, taking a sip of her coffee.

"Too hot," she said as she put it down.

She fiddled with the radio and found the Coyote, more old rock. We passed a sign warning that we needed chains or snow tires.

"Are these snow tires? We've been climbing, That's not the first time I've seen that sign."

"They're a regular year-round tire, but we can use four-wheel drive if we need to."

"How do I do that?"

"Push that button above the radio, the one that says 4x4. But not unless we get stuck. Swede always said you should slow down and stay in two-wheel drive. Save the four-wheel for if you get into trouble."

Another sign warned that bridges might be icy when *dry*, not just if they were wet. We were climbing so hard, Shenia had to downshift. There weren't any other vehicles on the road in either direction. The sky off to the north was glowing slightly, like maybe there was a city out there somewhere.

Alone like that with the girl I'd been liking for so long, you'd think I could have thought of something to say, but I was too heavy inside. It pulled me down against the window and I drifted off again.

-22-

Shenia's father pulled his wife's suitcase out of her car.

"Where are they?" she demanded. She picked up a large Macy's bag and closed the hatch. She automatically hit lock and the car chirped.

"We still don't know."

She straightened and held her jaw firmly. He knew this meant she was fighting tears. He'd seen it often enough when their son was flirting with gang activity.

"We should have moved out of this neighborhood years ago," she complained.

"I know," he replied.

"Your mother would have survived just as long if we'd moved to a good neighborhood. She didn't have to stay in this house."

"I know." It was a familiar conversation.

"Antoine never would have gotten into trouble. You would still be a detective."

He put his free arm around her. "I know."

"Are they sure he killed her?"

"No, the coroner hasn't worked on her yet."

"But you know she was killed."

"The coroner will be able to confirm that, but the bruising looked like someone forced her to take the pills."

"And you think it was the boy Shenia's been flirting with?"

"The neighbor heard him shouting at his mother last night."

"There's no one else it could be?"

"There was a boyfriend, but no one has seen him in months. And if the boy didn't do it, why would they run?" He sighed.

"What else? I know there's more you're not saying. Tell me."

"The uniform told me. Schuster's trying to keep me out of it."

"What?"

"There were other bruises and scars where they wouldn't show, some old, some new."

She sucked in a breath and grasped her husband's hand. He was her lifeline.

-23-

This was crazy.

He'd driven clear across Nevada for nothing. He'd been driving fast to catch up and hadn't seen them since the bus station. They weren't headed for the grandparents.

Maybe the little brat didn't say anything until they were in Reno. That made sense. That oldest kid would be looking to avenge his mama. He wouldn't run away.

They were headed back to Sacramento.

He pulled into the next rest area to sleep. He'd head back when he woke up. Even if they talked to the cops before he got to them, all he had to do was eliminate the little girl.

"I need to pee." It was Missy. The blinding light of the tunnel had woken her up. "I need to pee right now."

"There's a rest area in a couple miles, at the top of this," Shenia told her quietly, trying to let the boys continue sleeping.

They were climbing again, with bushes and small trees visible along the sides of the highway. Shenia read a sign to take Missy's mind off her need for a bathroom. "Silverzone Pass. 5940 feet. We're more than a mile higher than the ocean, Missy."

At the summit she pulled into an empty parking area with lights as bright as the tunnel had been. The boys still didn't wake up.

"Where are we?" Missy asked.

"Almost to Utah."

"That's way away from home, isn't it?"

"Yes, but you'll be okay. Put your hat on, honey." The wind bit right through Shenia's jacket. She yawned and a cloud formed in front of her mouth. She grabbed Missy's hand and they trotted to one of the unisex doors. Shenia searched for a switch inside the cold little building, but there was only a skylight. "I'll stay in here with you."

"There's cold air coming out of the toilet," Missy complained.

"It's a pit toilet, an outhouse. The wind must come in through ventilation. Just do your business as fast as you can."

When they got back into the car, Shenia cranked the heat.

"Put your seatbelt back on, Missy," she directed.

"Aren't you sleepy?" Missy asked.

She yawned and that made Shenia yawn, too. No one would see them here, but it was too cold. Besides, she wanted to get them as far from Sacramento as she could.

"I can make it awhile longer."

"I'll stay awake to keep you up," Missy promised.

But within a few minutes, Shenia was listening to the soft sounds of three sleeping passengers. It had been a tough day for them. They needed the sleep. Speeding through the dark, it felt as if she were driving a spaceship through the void.

Thursday: On the Run

-25-

He turned the car on again to warm up. He stretched his neck to get the kinks out. The sky was starting to get light. He'd had enough sleep. He needed to get back to Sacramento.

Then he saw the Explorer, parked across the lot from him, the only other car. He drove to the far end, past the restroom building, and parked where he could watch but not be easily seen. The two little kids got out and headed towards him by themselves.

This was his chance. He pulled up his hood, put on sunglasses, and hurried to the restroom building. There was a brick windbreak that hid the fact he went into the women's side.

-26-

The car door closing woke me up.

Jimmy was holding Missy's hand, taking her to the restroom. They were wearing their coats and the beanies we'd picked up with the groceries.

Shenia had tilted her seat back and was sleeping with her face up and her mouth open. The corner where her lips met was shiny with drool. She probably wouldn't like a picture of that, but it made me smile.

I pushed my tongue along the roof of my mouth to my teeth, trying to get some saliva going. It didn't do much. There was a bottle of water on the floor of the back seat that I managed to reach without disturbing Shenia. I took a swig and swished it around my mouth, then chugged it all down. Man, I'd been dehydrated.

I'd been using my new coat for a pillow. I got out of the car and slipped it on fast with my back to the wind, then pulled my hood up from inside of it. My new gloves and beanie were still in the back. I didn't want to open and close another door and wake up Shenia, so I shoved my hands into my pockets.

There was one truck with its engine running, over away from the auto parking and one car way down at the other end of the our lot. Most people probably stayed in motels when it was this cold.

I met Jimmy outside the restroom building, near a map of Utah.

"Did you stay up all night?" he asked.

"Nah. Shenia drove way past midnight, though. We better let her sleep some more."

"Are you going to drive?"

"Maybe later, but I don't want to wake her up to do it." Maybe I wanted to put it off, too. "Where's Missy?"

He shoved his jaw towards the door into the women's restroom. "I waited out here like Shenia said to do at the gas station, but I really need to pee, too."

"I'll wait for her. Go on."

-27-

He was so close.

She was right there in another stall. He'd started to position himself where he could grab her from behind when she came out. He'd cover her mouth so she couldn't scream, so he could get her to the car before the younger boy knew there was anything wrong, but then he heard them talking outside.

He couldn't take on the older boy, especially with the younger kids there to help. He slipped back into the end stall quietly. At least he knew where they were now. He could stay put until they moved away from the restrooms. Eventually he'd catch her alone.

Jimmy came out the same time as Missy.

"Come on, let's see what's at the top of this tower," said Jimmy.

It was more like a cement ramp than a tower. I watched with my hands in my jacket pockets while Jimmy ran ahead, then came back and bounced around Missy, then trotted backwards up the ramp, chattering to her the whole time. He needed to burn off the energy.

Outside the building, there were freebie newspapers for motels in Salt Lake City and other things we wouldn't need. I glanced back at the kids before going inside.

It was heated! That felt good. When I was done, I warmed my hands under the dryer, then went back outside. The chilling breeze hit me as soon as I stepped away from the building. I shoved my hands back into my coat pockets. The kids were on one of the cement benches, Missy leaning against Jimmy. I sat down next to her. Sitting on that bench was like sitting on an ice cube.

Then Missy climbed up onto my lap and snuggled into me like she used to when she was little. She had her fist against her mouth, chewing on the back of a finger through her mitten. Guess she was wanting to suck her thumb, but she'd given that up long ago.

She was taking Mama's death so hard. I wrapped my arms around her and rested my chin on the top of her head.

Without Missy against him, Jimmy got up and roamed around. He checked out the whole area, then came back to us. He had a white stone in his hand. There were a bunch of them on the ground. He stuck his tongue out against it.

"Jimmy, what are you doing?" I demanded. "You're not some little baby. What are you doing licking a rock?"

He tossed the stone away.

"Plaque over there says the Bonneville Salt Flats are across the highway, where they race cars," he said. "I thought it was like a chunk of salt, but it didn't taste salty. They're in the cement they used for the ramp, too."

"What else did you find?"

"There's another plaque that says the first transcontinental telephone line came together near here, and there's that map by the restroom with a bunch of information. It says that mountain driving may be hazardous during winter storms."

"We have the four wheel drive. We'll be fine. Besides, the first week of November isn't winter. This is just what fall feels like where it gets really cold."

Then Jimmy plopped down next to us. He grabbed the bench on either side of his legs. He'd thought to put on his gloves. He squeezed himself tight and rocked and stared at the sun starting to slide up into the sky. Two engines coupled together passed by on the railroad tracks.

"I wish Mama could see this," said Missy.

"Me too." I kissed the top of her head and she sighed.

We sat there as the sun slipped up, then disappeared behind clouds. It took some time, but it finally got up to where the yellow shine came through a crack in the gray.

It was good, sitting there, missing Mama with each other. We talked some about the happy times, mostly back when Swede was alive. My nose was cold, but I'd finally thought to pull my hands up inside my sleeves and Missy was warm on my lap.

"Remember how we'd go up into the mountains at Christmas and sled?" Jimmy asked.

"I don't remember that," pouted Missy.

"Sure you do. Mama sewed a ribbon between your mittens, and ran it through your coat, so you couldn't lose them. Remember?"

"My puppy mittens."

"That's right."

"They got too little for me, when we still lived in our old house." She heaved a big sigh. "I wish we'd never moved."

-29-

He eased his way out of the women's room and went back to his car. He couldn't snag her now, but he could go ahead, make sure he had plenty of gas, and be ready to follow when they came along the highway. There wasn't enough traffic out here to miss them, but they'd never notice him in his sister's car. They'd never seen it.

-30-

When Shenia woke up, we ate at a table that was partially sheltered from the icy wind. Shenia looked dead beat.

"Sure you don't want something?" I asked.

She shook her head, then put it down on the table like a little kid, on her crossed arms, and fell back asleep. Missy and Jimmy were quiet without my saying anything. It didn't take long for us to finish our food. Only after they were back in the car did I go to Shenia and gently shake her shoulder. Touching her while she was asleep like that made something inside me kinda tumble around.

"Sorry to wake you up, but we need to get on the road... unless you think we should only drive at night."

"I thought about that after you were all asleep." She yawned wide and kept her eyes half closed as she pulled her legs out from under the picnic table.

She grabbed hold of my arm to pull herself up. It couldn't possibly have done the same thing to her as it did to me.

She let go, stretched, and started for the car, still talking slow. "With the police in it, we should get as far as we can right away. There wasn't an Amber Alert, so the farther east we get, the less likely we'll be in the news. There's no reason for them to think you're headed this way, is there?"

"I don't think so. Mama never talked about her family. *I* didn't even know where they were until I saw that envelope."

"That message last night was weird. But at least there's someone who wants to hear from you." She tilted her head and I heard her neck crack. "You should call again. It's not so early there."

"The kids are ready to go. I'll do that when you stop for gas."

"When *you* stop for gas." She dropped the keys in my hand.

The car looked lived in with the blankets we'd bought. Shenia got into the passenger seat and pulled one of them over her with some of it bunched up between her head and the window. Jimmy and Missy already had their seatbelts on and neither of them said a word as I moved the driver's seat back, then stuffed my legs under the steering wheel.

"You need any help this time?" Shenia yawned.

I checked. She had her seatbelt on, too.

"No, it was just I couldn't see last night."

She nodded and settled against her window. I hit lock for all the doors, put the key in the ignition, adjusted the mirrors, and started the Explorer. I gently curved back and out of the parking place. There were a few other cars at the rest stop now, but none moving.

First to second the car revved enough I knew I was giving it too much gas and taking too long, second to third went easier and I moved right onto the highway. A truck came up behind me kind of fast, but he moved over and passed. I held onto the steering wheel tight and focused far ahead in my lane and tried not to look at that wall moving by us. Then he was past us and I shifted into fourth, then fifth, without a hitch.

A sign said it was 111 miles to Salt Lake City.

Shenia leaned over and looked at the trip meter. "I meant to stop at Wendover for gas, but I was so tired I missed it. You better take the first exit that has fuel."

She was right, we were almost on empty. The next exit said no services. It was pretty desolate country. Every so often there was a warning for drowsy drivers to pull over if necessary.

"Should I turn around and go back to that town you missed?"

Shenia looked in the atlas. Good thing I'd thought to get it.

"No, it's too far now. Just take the next exit."

But that one said no services, too. And the next one. The needle dropped down below the E. I looked at Shenia. I couldn't say what I was thinking without scaring the kids, but Shenia understood. If we ran out of gas, we'd have to get help, and help might get us stopped and taken back to where they'd split us up.

That couldn't happen. We couldn't have that much bad luck.

If we could just get to our grandparents, once they saw the kids, they'd keep them. But over the phone, across the country, it would be way too easy for them to say no. We had to make it to them.

When I finally saw an exit with a gas station, I realized I'd been holding my breath. The car took more than it was supposed to hold. Maybe Mama *was* watching out for us.

"She'd have answered if *I* had called," Shenia's mother told her husband over breakfast.

"Not if he isn't letting her."

Unhappy with that thought, she changed the subject. "What was the phone call while I was in the shower? Is there any news?"

"They got a signal on the phones, tracked them to the back of a farmer's truck in Vacaville. The kids obviously dumped them."

"Well, where had he been?

"He came in from Nevada last night. Says his last stop was Reno. So we believe they're headed east along I-80."

"Is the Amber Alert out?"

"No. They don't believe it's an abduction. The kids and Shenia showed no signs of being forced into the car."

"Well, what's being done to find them then? And don't you dare tell me we're waiting for twenty-four hours to pass."

"No, their pictures went out over NCIC as persons of interest in a possible homicide."

"All of them? That makes them sound like suspects."

"The older boy *is* a suspect. And other police departments will watch for them more actively this way. Some states don't do much with runaways." He got up and gave his wife a quick peck on the cheek. "Try not to worry. I'll call if there's any news."

Shenia studied the map while I added oil again.

"Do you think you can drive through Salt Lake City? It'll be ten by the time we get there, well past rush hour."

I wasn't really sure, but she still looked tired, so I said, "I'm good. Jimmy can watch signs for me."

"And I want you to stop near a motel, where I can get a signal. I should email my daddy, let him know I'm okay, and send him looking the wrong direction."

"I'll get off at the first exit past Salt Lake City that has hotels."

Shenia stayed awake for maybe three seconds after I got back on the highway. The road was elevated and we were driving with water on both sides.

"Is that salt stuck to those fence posts in the water?" asked Jimmy.

"I think so," I told him. "I'm not sure if we're in the middle of Great Salt Lake, but we're close, anyway."

Jimmy checked the map. "We're right at the south end of the lake. Wow, it's like a mirror."

The mountains and sky reflected in the water crystal clear. And there were mountains ahead that looked like they'd been chopped off, until I saw one hazy mountaintop showing through the mist and realized it was clouds hiding the peaks.

"Those mountains are huge," said Jimmy.

"Is that snow?" Missy asked.

There was a dusting of white on some of the peaks.

"Yeah, I think it is."

As long as the snow was up there and not down on the road, it didn't matter. Sometimes we could see snow on the mountains when it was warm in Sacramento.

"Look at the castle!" said Missy. "It's got shiny kisses on top."

Off to the left was a building with those round-topped towers like you see on pictures from the Middle East. I wasn't sure why there'd be one here. All I remembered about Utah was that it was the center of the Mormon religion.

"They do look like Hershey's kisses." I brought my eyes back to the road and kept them there.

Traffic was getting a little heavier. There still wasn't much, though. It was nothing compared to Sacramento, and Jimmy was enjoying being navigator. He was reading all the signs, every single one of them.

Shenia woke up as I got into the city. "You're doing great."

"Thanks. It's not hard now I can see."

"Cop ahead on the right," Jimmy announced.

"I'm going the speed limit," I told him. "Duck down so he doesn't see you kids."

Jimmy and Missy laid their heads down on the seat until Shenia told them we were clear.

"If they're looking for us we should swap these plates for some from another Explorer. From another state's the best," said Jimmy.

"What kind of movies have you been watching?" Shenia teased.

Jimmy laughed, then stopped suddenly. "Michael, he pulled out. He's following us."

I checked in the mirror. Jimmy wasn't joking.

"His lights aren't on; he's probably done with his shift is all, or maybe it's his meal break." But Shenia sounded like she was trying to convince herself, then she said, "Take the next exit, just in case."

I signaled, then took the exit and turned right toward some motels.

"He turned on his flashers!" Shenia cried. "He's taking the exit."

I pulled into the first motel and around behind it. There were several cars in the lot. I parked next to a Chevy Bronco from Kansas.

"I'm switching plates," I said as I jumped out of the car.

Jimmy was over the seat and had two screwdrivers out before I opened the back.

"Take off our rear plate first," I told him. "Keep them with us."

When I came back with the Chevy plate, he was already at the front of the Explorer. As I finished tightening the last screw, he brought our second plate around and tossed it into the car with the other one.

"The Bronco doesn't have a front plate," he told me.

"Some states only have one on the back," said Shenia.

She had her hand out.

"Give me the keys and climb in, Michael. I'll pull the cover over you. Jimmy, get in the back seat with Missy. She's on the floor. I'll put a blanket over the two of you, too. It'll look like I'm alone."

I laid down with the bags and cooler and she threw a blanket over me, then pulled the cover back.

Shenia slammed the hatch shut and I could hear her covering up the kids. Two more door slams. I heard the driver's seat move, and then she started the car.

"Everyone stay quiet and still until I tell you it's all clear," she said.

-33-

"I've got a green Explorer at the light. It's about to get onto the highway going east. She pulled up next to me," the officer said into his radio. "It looks like the same car, but she's alone."

"Any chance the others are in the car?"

"Can't see anyone else, but it looks like there's a bunch of blankets and stuff in the back. They could be hiding."

"Does she fit the description?"

"Yes. But she doesn't look nervous. She's getting something out of her eye, checking her makeup in her visor mirror."

"Follow her anyway."

"Should I pull her over?"

"Not until you check the plate. If it's not them, we don't want to be slammed for racial profiling."

The left turn arrow turned green.

Shenia flipped up the visor and entered the ramp for the highway. She glanced in the rearview mirror.

The police car was still sitting at the light.

"She pulled onto the freeway. Kansas plate, not California."

"Okay, cruise the area, see if you can spot them."

-34-

The kids were running from the cops!

There was nothing to worry about after all. He lost them when they turned into that motel and the cop came down the street, but that didn't matter. He could go home to Sacramento and rest easy. They'd never go back if they were hiding from the police.

She must not have seen him after all.

That kid would be after him if she had.

-35-

We were a half hour out of the city, headed into more mountains on a six-lane highway with little traffic when Shenia pulled off and stopped in the parking lot of a motel that advertised free Wi-Fi. The kids and Shenia piled out of the car. Jimmy came around and opened the hatch for me. Snowcapped mountains towered above us. It wasn't a dusting on them here, and it was freezing. I pulled on my winter jacket and dug out my new hat and gloves.

"Why don't you and the kids stretch while I check my email and the weather," Shenia said. "Get the kinks out."

"I'm fine," I told her. "Jimmy, see if you can find a restroom for Missy. Stay together, though."

"We know. You don't have to keep saying it," said Jimmy.

I gave him an apology smile and then walked around to the passenger seat, where Shenia had settled in with her laptop.

"You really had a cop sitting right next to us?" I asked.

"Yeah. Good thing we switched the plates. That little brother of yours is something else."

"Yeah." I sighed. I was going to have to talk to him about stealing that plate. We'd had to do it, but it was up to me to make sure he knew it was still wrong.

I wanted to see what Shenia was doing, but her computer screen was tilted away from the door. I closed it and walked around to the driver's seat and got in out of the cold, though the car was chilling down awfully fast. When I turned to talk to her, she'd shifted position so the screen was turned away from me again.

"Where were you fourth period yesterday?" she asked.

"Why?"

"My father says you were marked absent fourth period."

"I came in late because I'd been down in the guidance office talking to Mr. Roberts. I had a pass... But why does your father care what I was doing in school?"

"So if he talks to Mr. Roberts, they can clear that up?"

"Why does it need to be cleared up?"

She didn't answer.

"Sure, Mr. Roberts keeps a schedule of who he's talking to. Why are they asking so many questions?" Suddenly I knew. "They don't think it was suicide, do they." It wasn't really a question.

"No," she said. "There was milk all over the kitchen like someone had gotten mad and thrown it, and there wasn't any on her."

"I did that," I interrupted. "When I went back in for the keys. It was sitting on the shelf going bad, with a bunch of other groceries."

"She got a job yesterday morning, Michael. The neighbor said she was happy as could be when she got home."

"But the note?"

"They think someone made her write it, made her swallow those pills."

"Lester," I wanted to go take care of him myself, right now.

"Her old boyfriend?"

"Yeah."

"He's their other suspect, but no one's seen him around for weeks."

"Other?"

"When they get to Mr. Roberts, they'll know you were at school."

"They think I did that to Mama?" I felt like my whole body could explode into pieces.

Shenia reached out and put a hand on my arm. "Only because they don't know where you were, and no one's seen her old boyfriend."

"You knew in Reno that they thought I killed her?"

"I knew it was a mistake."

"You took off with us, helped us get away..."

"I knew they were wrong."

Tears poured down my face like a faucet had been turned on. Shenia reached out and held my hand and that made them come harder. Then I saw the kids headed back to the car and pulled my hand away to wipe my face off quick while I snuffed it up.

"You gonna tell your father to talk to Mr. Roberts?" I asked.

"Yeah."

"He must be going nuts, thinking you might be with a killer. Tell him we're taking the kids to their grandparents, and that he better find Lester before I get back there."

"Well, I won't put it that way."

"Put it however you want, he'd better find Lester before I do."

"What's his last name? Do you know where he lives?"

"I didn't pay much attention. He was living with us and working nights stocking at Walmart. I'm not sure which one. Don't know where he went when she kicked him out."

Jimmy and Missy bounced into the back seat.

"It's cold!" Missy said.

"Did you check the weather and road conditions?" asked Jimmy. "The sign back at the rest area said it's udot.utah.gov."

"Soon as I send this email," said Shenia.

"Are you letting your daddy know you're okay?" asked Missy.

"Yes, honey." She pushed send, then signed off her email. "Okay, udot.utah.gov."

Jimmy hung over her shoulder while she pushed keys. I turned on the car to get the heater going. I didn't like to waste the gas, but the windows were frosting with our warm breath.

"It looks like this is all about accidents in the city. Let me try this link to weather.gov... Oh no."

"What?" Not more bad news, please.

"My battery died. There's no way to charge it in this car, either... but if there was a major problem, it would have been on that page, I think."

I hoped she was right.

"Say, Shenia, did we go by Area 51 last night?" Jimmy asked.

"Don't know; it wasn't labeled if we did," she told him.

"There was one spot where I saw a weird glow off to the north," I teased. But he didn't realize I was kidding, so I said, "Might have been a base or something."

"Cool."

Schuster was sitting at his desk when Brown came up and handed him the email from Shenia.

"She says they're headed for the grandparents in Colorado."

"Do you believe her?" asked Schuster.

"They're probably going any other direction. She obviously believes the boy. She says he was with the guidance counselor when he was marked absent, a Mr. Roberts. She insists he'd never hurt his mother. Oh, and the boy says he spilled the milk before they left."

"Threw it is more like it," said Schuster.

Brown nodded. He'd been the first to see that kitchen. "And he says it had to have been the boyfriend, Lester. Says he works night shift at a Walmart. What do you think?"

"You aren't on this case."

"I'm helping you communicate with them. Do you think that boy murdered his mother?"

"We'll check with the counselor. Did you send the email to the geeks? Maybe they can figure out where she was when she sent it."

"Yes, I sent it to the geeks. What do you think about the boy? Is he still your primary? My daughter is with those kids."

"All the more reason for you to keep out of it. You know that."

"I know the coroner's report says it was murder and that the neighbor heard the boy shouting at his mother the night before she died."

"You know too much."

"Tell me if you think my daughter's with a killer!"

Heads turned to see Brown leaning over his fisted hands toward the seated detective. He realized what he was doing and pulled back.

Schuster sighed and ran a hand across the top of his head where his hair used to be. He waited until everyone turned back to their work, then answered quietly. "I don't think so. According to school, the kid's not a discipline problem, and the neighbor was shocked the argument makes him a suspect. She thinks Mom was seeing someone while the kids were in school—she heard things that didn't sound like television. She thinks it may have been the old boyfriend, but she never spotted him."

"She didn't mention that when I interviewed her."

"Maybe you stopped asking questions when she described your daughter."

Brown's shoulders dropped and his hands opened as he sighed.

"You're right. I just hope you're right about the boy, too."

Schuster put the email into a folder and picked up another case that needed his attention. Brown was still standing there. The poor guy had been through enough with his son. He didn't need to be this worried about his daughter. Schuster put the work down and spoke softly.

"We're thinking the same as the kid. Fingerprints upstairs are from an ex-con, Lester Madden and we got a positive ID from the neighbor; he's the boyfriend the victim kicked out last summer. He's not the kind of guy to take that well. He was in prison for domestic assault."

"Have you questioned him?" asked Brown.

"He quit his last known job. The apartment is his listed address."

"How about his parole officer?"

"Doesn't have one. Did his full time. We're tracking down a sister. So leave it to us now. Stay out of it. You'll be the first to know when we find the kids."

-37-

"According to the atlas mileage map, it's about six hours to Cheyenne and another eight to Omaha," said Jimmy.

He was now the official navigator. The atlas was keeping him busier than the video game he'd bought for a dollar.

"We went through Salt Lake about ten this morning, didn't we?" asked Shenia.

"Yep. So we should be in Cheyenne by four this afternoon, Omaha by midnight. Then it's Friday, and it's eight and a half hours to Chicago, so that'll be about eight thirty in the morning, and then it's six hours to Cleveland, which means..." Jimmy counted it off on his fingers. "Two thirty in the afternoon and the last part I have to guess, but about an hour or two later we'll be there. If you guys keep driving the whole time, we'll be there tomorrow afternoon."

"That's the plan," I told him.

I wanted to get the kids set with their grandparents and then Shenia and I were heading back to California. Lester wasn't going to get away with this.

"We're going to change time zones again," Shenia reminded us. "So it's going to be two hours later than you were figuring. It'll be evening when we get there. You should really call that woman again, Michael."

"What woman?" Jimmy asked.

"We're not sure. It's supposed to be your grandparents' number, but we're pretty sure it was a black woman who left the message," Shenia explained.

"Our grandma's black?" Missy asked.

"I thought you were asleep," I said.

"Our dad must have had some strong genes for us to end up this blonde," Jimmy said.

"I don't think so," I told him. "I think the message was left by a friend or something."

"Could it be one of your father's relatives, Michael?" Shenia asked.

"I doubt it," I said.

"Call and find out," said Jimmy.

"Fine. But not right now. The next time we stop," I told him.

Talking on a cell phone while you drive is illegal in California. I wasn't sure about other states, but I wanted to play it safe. Besides, I wasn't all that comfortable behind the wheel yet anyway.

"Hey! We're in Wyoming!"

"Don't yell like that while I'm driving, Jimmy."

He got a little quieter, but not much. "There's visitor information ahead. Stop there, Michael. You can call and maybe we can get some maps and stuff."

"We'll never get there if we keep stopping," I complained.

"I need to pee."

"Missy, you're just saying that." She never went this often.

"I want to find out if our grandma's black," she said.

"Fine, I'll stop."

It was a state park information center, right off the highway. The kids went into the building while Shenia looked for the number.

She started digging through her backpack. "I know I had it written down on a piece a paper, not just in the phone we ditched."

"You could find it again online if you have to, couldn't you?"

"If there's a place to charge my computer, and Wi-Fi." She pulled out the map to Reno and flipped it over. "Here it is."

I took it and opened the prepaid phone. "I'll save it on here, so we don't have to worry about it again."

"Are you getting a signal?"

"Yeah, not very strong, though. Only two bars."

"Call."

I dialed the number and waited while it connected, then started counting the rings. It went into voicemail again, but it was a different message. I switched to speaker phone right away so Shenia could hear it without burning minutes twice.

"Michael, I am so glad to hear from you, but I couldn't get your number to work. I've got a doctor's appointment in Erie today, so you'll have to call after seven this evening. Don't call too late, though; I'm an old lady. I need to talk to your mother, too."

I turned to Shenia. "I can't tell her what happened on the phone. She might have a heart attack. We'd never find out who she is."

"You can say your mama's not with you, not say why. You're sure that's not your grandmother?"

"I'm not sure of anything anymore."

Jimmy and Missy came out then. Jimmy had a stack of brochures and stuff.

"Is she our grandma?" Missy asked.

"She wasn't there," Shenia answered.

Maybe I'd misunderstood about that phone call when my daddy died. I was awfully little. But no, when we argued the other night, Mama said they cut her off because she hooked up with my father. She didn't come out and say it, but I was sure it was because he was black. The woman on the phone couldn't be her mother.

"Can we eat something?" Jimmy, of course.

We needed to be driving. Besides, it was even colder here than it had been in Utah, way too cold to sit at a picnic table.

"Pull the cooler up behind the seat," I told him. "You can eat in the car. Just try not to make a mess. And you have to have your seatbelt on while we're moving."

"Let me make a sandwich first."

"Okay."

"I'll drive for a while so you can eat," Shenia offered. "You can call again around five or six. That'll be seven or eight her time. Let her know we'll be there tomorrow night."

Shenia and Jimmy were good with all their calculations, but none of them meant a thing.

-38-

Shenia's mother pushed food around her dinner plate with her fork.

"It was definitely murder?" she asked.

"Yes, the coroner says someone forced the pills down her throat."

"And they're not sure whether the boy did it or not?"

"They're pretty sure it was the ex-boyfriend."

"But they still don't know where the boy was?" she asked.

"No, they don't know for sure. They're having trouble reaching the counselor. He took some personal time."

"Do you think we should tell Antoine what's happening?"

"No." Antoine was in the service now, stationed in the thick of things. He needed to focus on where he was and what he was doing. He didn't tell his mother as much as he did his father. He never had.

"I think we should," she insisted. "He can add his prayers to ours."

"Please don't. They don't think the boy did it."

"But they're not sure, and why else would he run?" She put her fork down. She didn't expect an answer. "I knew Shenia was falling for him. I should have insisted on her bringing him over sooner, but I was hoping it would fade out."

"Because he lives in the apartments?"

"Don't make it sound like I'm a snob. You know where you get most of your police calls. Even if he didn't kill his mother, the woman was murdered and he undoubtedly witnessed her being abused before that. I don't want our daughter caught up in that cycle."

"Okay, okay." He put his hands up. "You're right. I want a better life for Shenia, too. But everything that they've heard about the boy is positive, except that he shouted at his mother the night before she died."

"Exactly."

"How often would a neighbor hear us shouting if we shared walls?"

"Why Utah?" she asked to change the subject. "That couldn't have been them."

"It fits with their having been through Reno. We'll know if they manage to track the path of her email."

"If you're right and they're heading east, they'll either stay on eighty or drop down to seventy. Either one's going to be bad."

"I know."

Brown wished he hadn't told her about the police spotting in Salt Lake. The first thing she did was check the weather. A major storm was swooping down from Canada across the Rockies.

Shenia had never driven in winter conditions.

-39-

"Is it snowing?" asked Missy.

It was hard to be sure at first. The flakes were so tiny, it could have been a trick of the light, but it was snow. I'd dozed off against the window. A glance at the clock told me it hadn't been an hour.

"You ever driven in the mountains in winter?" I asked Shenia.

"No. My folks don't care much for cold."

"That one time Swede took me out to drive, it was in this big gravel parking lot, and he had me stomp on the brakes and that loose gravel made the rear end fish back and forth all over the place. He made me practice straightening it out. Said it was like driving on ice."

"Well, this stuff's melting. There's no ice."

"Watch the bridges, though. Remember all those signs."

"Michael!" Missy tapped my shoulder. "Look at the mountains!" She rapped on the glass by my head. "Look!"

Way off to the south there were mountains that made everything else we'd seen look small, and they were coated in white.

"That must be the Rockies, Missy."

"That's snow?"

"Yep."

"What are those fences for?" asked Jimmy.

There were fences on either side of the road, parallel rows of them stretching across wide empty fields.

"I don't know. They wouldn't keep anything in, that's for sure."

"Look, fifty-cent ice cream," said Missy.

There were billboards for Little America, a lot of them.

"That looks like a big travel plaza," I said. "We can get gas there, if you want ice cream."

Shenia pulled into the place. There were new, polished, monster SUVs and pretend colonial buildings with no one in sight. We looked at each other, then Shenia turned right around and left.

"Someone would notice us there," I told Missy.

"That's okay. It's too cold for ice cream," she said.

But I gave Jimmy money so they could get a treat when we stopped at the Flying J a little further on, in Rock Springs. It was a truck stop that looked like a truck stop—big, busy, with all kinds of people coming and going. No one paid any attention to us. I remembered to check the oil. It needed another quart, but the other fluids were okay.

"We'll be fine even if we get into heavier snow, right? With the four-wheel drive?" Shenia asked while the kids were in the store.

"Yeah, we'll be fine. I'll drive."

She surprised me by not arguing.

As I pulled back onto the highway, Jimmy pointed at some more of those weird fences. "I asked in the store. They're snow fences. When it's windy they catch the snow and make it drift in the fields instead of on the road."

Those fences might catch some snow, but it was still blowing across the road so thick it was hard to see, and it felt like the car was getting pushed sideways, too. I had to slow down. We made it to Rawlins about half past four, a little later than Jimmy said we should. We were climbing, and the snow kept getting thicker, until it was really coming down and sticking. The winter speed limit was sixty-five, but the line of trucks I was following had dropped to forty-five and that seemed plenty fast to me. No one complained about the radio being off. We slowed down to forty.

"You need to put on your four-way flashers going this slow. So people coming up behind can see you," said Shenia.

"Who's going to go faster than this?"

"It's the law," said the policeman's daughter.

I put on the flashers.

Before long I was glad—a tanker truck zipped right by us. It was hard to see when he passed, but I still made out the flammable sign. We kept on heading up and where the incline was the steepest there was an extra lane, so the trucks weren't quite as close when they went by us. But the snow kept coming down harder until I wasn't sure how many lanes there were. I just followed the taillights of the truck ahead of me and hoped he stayed on the road.

Then another truck passed and it kicked up so much snow that I couldn't see at all. I couldn't see that truck, I couldn't see the lights of the one I'd been following or anything behind me—I couldn't even see the road or the markers along the edge. It was like the car was suddenly inside a big snowball. And there was enough snow on the road, I didn't hear the washboard at the edge of the pavement either, but when it finally cleared enough to see the taillights ahead of me, I realized I was on the shoulder. There had been steep drop-offs to the right earlier. There was no way to know what was out there now. Holding the wheel tight, I went just fast enough to not lose sight of the truck ahead of me. Those itty-bitty lights were the only way I knew which way the road was going. We hit another steep incline, which made him slow down more, but I had no interest in passing him. Unfortunately, other trucks wanted to keep up their speed and every time one passed, I held my breath and kept the wheel as steady as I could until I could see again. I didn't even glance at the clock. Time didn't matter. Staying on the road and staying alive was everything. Keeping the kids safe.

When I saw the blue rest area sign, I gave thanks in my heart that it wasn't covered in snow. No one made a sound until I'd backed into a parking place near the restroom building. With the lights in the parking lot, it didn't even look like it was snowing all that hard.

"Gimme the cell phone a minute," said Jimmy.

Shenia handed it back to him. He used it for a flashlight to check his mileage map. "That should have taken forty-five minutes, but it took almost two hours," he said.

I didn't care. We were safe.

"We're staying here for the night," I told them.

"Will we be warm enough?" asked Shenia.

"You take Missy into the bathroom. Jimmy and I will put all the stuff from the rear into the front and put the back seat down. If we sleep on the old blanket from the car and put the new ones over top of us and cuddle all together, we should be fine."

"Okay. Come on, Missy," said Shenia.

I hoped I was right.

"Who's going to sleep next to who?" Jimmy asked.

The girls were already inside the car. We were in the restroom, warming our hands back up under the dryers.

"I don't know. How do you want to do it?" I asked him.

"I'd rather sleep next to Missy, on the outside. You should sleep on the other outside, so the girls stay warm enough," Jimmy said.

"I guess." I wasn't sure how Shenia would feel about it, and I definitely wouldn't want to explain it to her father.

But when we got back, the girls had done it their own way. Shenia was on the outside and Missy was in the middle.

"We can use our packs for pillows," said Shenia. "We took your soccer ball out of yours, Jimmy. It's on the floor up front. You sleep next to Missy. Michael and I will keep you two warm."

I guess she was thinking the same way as Jimmy, only she saw us as the grownups taking care of the kids and he saw us as the men taking care of the girls. He did what she said, though. I was relieved. Next to Shenia, I'd never have slept. I'd have been too afraid of what might happen while I was dreaming.

"Where's the cell phone?" I asked.

"Here, it was in my pocket," said Jimmy.

We were all snuggled down for the night and it was barely seven o'clock. I tried calling that lady again, but we were in a dead area. It would have to wait until morning.

That was one of the longest nights of my life. For twelve hours we stayed there. Missy had to go pee twice, probably because it was still pretty cold. I thought to tell everyone to put their hats on sometime in the night, to keep warmer. It wasn't as bad as it could have been, though.

Outside it was frigid.

A few other cars came and went. Most of them kept running their engines to warm up. I'd heard about some kids who died that way when the tailpipe filled up with snow and the carbon monoxide got to them, so we didn't do that.

We were warm enough. I didn't even keep my gloves on.

The time I took Missy to the bathroom, there were a couple guys speaking Spanish where I was waiting for her. They spoke a few words of English and I spoke a few of Spanish and we all talked pretty good with our hands. They'd just gotten in and it was still bad. "No mira nada" when the trucks passed them.

They didn't even have winter coats on. I wished we had extras to share, but the kids came first.

Friday: Too Much

-40-

Sometime after six, it got light enough so the mercury vapor parking lot lights turned off. We all got up and got ready for the road. There wasn't any question about eating outside the car; it was still snowing. While everyone else waited in the restroom, I got the car started so it would warm up inside and I left it running while I cleared the snow off.

Most of it on the outside of the car brushed away easily with my arm, until I got to the windshield. The wipers were stuck onto the glass and there was a crusty layer over the center of it.

In Sacramento, the few times we got enough frost to have a problem, people either put their hair dryer on an extension cord to melt it, or they scraped it off with a credit card. We'd cut up Mama's credit card, but I had my school ID.

I was so focused on scraping with that little piece of plastic, I didn't see the guy come up with a proper scraper, one of the long ones with an icebreaker at one end and a brush at the other.

"Stand back so I don't get you covered in snow," he said.

His voice had a western twang and he was wearing jeans with cowboy boots and hat. And his jacket looked like real leather with a real wool lining. I did like he said while he cleaned off the car.

"Thanks," I said. "We don't get much snow where I live."

"I'll get your lights, too, front and back," the cowboy said.

My heart almost stopped when he brushed off the Kansas plate, but he didn't seem to notice. I was pretty sure it snowed in Kansas.

"They may have sold out of these at the next gas station," he said. "I've got an extra in my truck. You keep this one."

"Thanks."

"You should use it on the inside of your back window, too, where it's all frosted up."

"Thank you. Drive safe."

He was gone before Shenia and the kids came back.

"I wish we really were going to get there tonight," I said.

"No chance of that. I heard a couple truckers talking in there. It's all the way across Nebraska." Shenia looked worried.

"How long's it going to last?"

"They didn't say."

"We can't stay here."

"I can drive," she offered, but I could tell she didn't want to.

"The kids are my responsibility. I should drive."

She gave me a smile. "You were amazing last night. They said it's not quite as bad this morning."

"Let's hope they're right."

Once everyone was in the car, buckled in tight, I slowly pulled out of the parking space. I was glad I'd thought to back into it. I couldn't see much out the rear window. It was still frosty on the inside.

I stopped and put on the parking brake. No other cars were moving, so I left it right in the middle of the lot, got out, opened the back window, and scraped the inside like the man had said I should. It might fog up again, but I'd be able to see a little better for now.

I accelerated like a turtle as we went up the on-ramp, timing it so I'd come onto the highway between groups of semis. The first one to pass us didn't kick up much snow at all. There was still some coming down, but very little. There were even some bare places in the road where the snowplow had scraped it clean. The rest was packed hard.

Gradually I increased my speed until forty-five and even fifty was comfortable. Everyone else was going faster, but visibility was good and they weren't blinding me when they passed, so that wasn't a problem. There was a sign saying thirty miles to Laramie when I hit a patch of ice.

I never had a chance to correct. One moment we were fine, the next we were sideways in the road, heading for one of those little reflector stakes between us and the median strip.

I think I managed to miss the reflector, though we'd never have felt it anyway. As we left the road, the car tilted to the point where it was going to roll, but I turned the nose downhill and we didn't go over. I must have closed my eyes, because the next thing I saw was the lanes of oncoming traffic right ahead of us. I turned the wheel hard and braked and we finished our slide facing the way we'd come from, the back end of the car a few yards from the westbound lanes.

"Whoa, we were airborne!" said Jimmy.

He didn't seem to understand that was not a good thing.

"Then we almost rolled!" he shouted.

"Jimmy, please be quiet, I really need it to be quiet right now." My voice sounded strained even to me, like Mama's had when we'd pushed her too far or when something else had her seriously upset.

I took a breath and relaxed my shoulders. Then I pushed the 4x4 button. The car moved through the snow easily. The ground must have frozen first, or we'd be stuck in mud. The snow was up to the bottom of the door, but fluffy, puffing up as I drove through it slowly. There was a sharp incline slightly higher than the car between us and the road. I stayed back and waited until no one was coming, then slow and steady drove up that slope and onto the highway.

If we'd gone off completely sideways, we *would* have rolled.

Back on the interstate, I pulled into the slow lane and put on my flashers and stayed as far right as I could and still be on the road. Whenever someone passed me, I eased off onto the shoulder. Those thirty miles took us over an hour, but we got to Laramie in one piece. I drove to the first motel and parked.

"What are you doing?" asked Shenia.

"I'm getting a room," I said.

"It's still morning," said Jimmy.

"I'm getting a room," I repeated. "Wait in the car."

"But..."

I ignored him and got out and slammed the door. Shenia caught up to me before I could get into the office.

"What about getting the kids to their grandparents?"

"I almost killed the kids back there, in case you didn't notice."

I was angry now. Angry at everything that had happened in the last two days, angry at Lester, angry that our only relatives were strangers, angry at the weather, angry at myself for taking this foolish trip, and I was angry at Shenia for encouraging me to do it.

"We're okay," she said.

"But we all could have been killed. Because I'm not supposed to be driving and no one should be driving in this stupid weather on icy roads with crazy truck drivers."

"Okay, if you need to stop for a night, we can do that. I'll take the kids down to that side door so they don't see all of us. Maybe the storm will pass tonight. We'll get an early start tomorrow."

"No. I'm calling that woman until I get hold of her and I'm going to get an adult to take responsibility for the kids. I can't do it." I started shaking. "I can't do it. I can't even take care of myself, let alone them. I'm getting a room."

"At least wait until you're not so upset before you call, Michael."

"Fine. I will. Now let me take care of this."

"Why's Michael making us stop here?" demanded Jimmy. "Why don't you drive?"

"He needs a break," Shenia answered. "And he's right. If I'd been driving, we'd probably have rolled, and it wouldn't do us any good to get into an accident. Even if we didn't get hurt, we'd end up sent back."

"No!" cried Missy.

"Okay," said Jimmy.

"You'll let Michael rest here awhile, so he'll feel okay driving again?"

Both kids nodded.

"We can't go back," said Missy.

"Once he's calmed down, he's going to call that lady who knows your grandparents," said Shenia. "Who knows? Maybe they'll send some money for bus tickets the rest of the way."

Of course, *she* would have to go back and face her parents.

-42-

Once we were in the motel room, I plopped face down on one of the beds. I pretended to be asleep long enough for it to become true. When I woke up, I was a lot more relaxed. Anyone could have hit an ice patch. But I still knew I wanted an adult to take charge.

"Where's the phone?" I asked.

The kids were watching cartoons. Shenia had her laptop plugged in and was busy on that. Jimmy reached into his pocket and handed me the prepaid phone.

"I'm going down to the lobby to call that lady."

"Can I go get some ice with you?" Jimmy asked.

Shenia looked up from the computer. "I wouldn't let them leave the room. I wasn't sure what you told the manager."

"I said there were four of us. He didn't ask whether it was adults or kids. But I'd rather you all stay in the room. Give me the ice bucket and I'll bring some back with me."

Surprisingly, no one argued.

There wasn't anyone in the lobby, not even the desk clerk. It sounded like he had a TV in a room out back. I went over to a chair in a corner and made the call. This time she was there.

"Michael?"

That's how she answered the phone, just my name, like it couldn't be anyone else calling her. It creeped me out a little, but I answered, "This is Michael."

"Michael Dolan McCarthy? Lynn Dolan's little boy?"

"I'm Lynn Marie Dolan McCarthy Johnson's son." That was a mouthful, but I wanted to make sure she knew who I was talking about. "Is this Michael Dolan's number? He's my grandfather."

"After all these years! Angelina had me keep this phone number so your mother could get through to her, if she ever called. I don't even give it out; my friends use my cell number."

Okay, so that's why she knew it would be me.

"Is my grandmother there?"

"Where are you, child?"

"We're in Laramie, Wyoming, on our way to see them."

Tough Times 91

"Let me talk to your mother."

"Uh, she couldn't come. It's just me and the kids."

"The kids?"

"My little brother and sister are with me."

"Lynnie has three children?" She sounded ready to burst with the excitement.

"Yes, ma'am," I said politely, but I was thinking who *are* you?

"Well, how old are you to be traveling all that way alone?"

"Jimmy's eleven, Missy's nine. A friend of mine and I are driving."

"I didn't realize you were already old enough to drive."

"Ma'am." I couldn't stand it anymore. "Who are you, please?"

"Maggie Hogan's my name."

"Could I speak to one of my grandparents, please?"

"They're not here."

"When will they be back?"

There was a pause, then she said, "They moved to California."

"They moved to California?" I couldn't have heard her right.

"Yes, they moved to Sacramento about seven years ago."

"Sacramento?" We'd almost been killed and for what? We'd been driving *away* from our grandparents!

"You have their old phone number?" I demanded.

"When I moved in here, your grandmother asked me to keep their phone line with a machine on it, so Lynnie would be able to find them."

"So you don't even know my mother?"

"Well, I never met her in the flesh, but your grandmother told me so much about her, I feel as if I was there the whole time she was growing up."

"She told you all about my mother because you were moving into their old house?"

"Oh, I wasn't a stranger. We were in a support group together, your grandmother and me, for years."

"A support group?"

"My daughter disappeared, too, from college."

"My mother didn't disappear."

"After your daddy died she did. She moved, forwarding address unknown. They had no idea where she'd gone. When my daughter showed up, it gave your grandmother hope."

"Why'd they move, if they were hoping she'd come back?" None of this made sense.

"Someone showed your grandma photos from their ski trip to Lake Tahoe, and she saw Lynnie in one of them."

"How could she be sure from one little photo?"

"You were with her and Lynnie was wearing a hat your grandma had knit for her, somewhere near the lake."

"At Christmas time?"

"I believe so."

Mama did always wear the same handmade yarn hat when we went up there. "So they just up and moved? Because of a picture? Why Sacramento? You said the picture was at Lake Tahoe."

"I think you were wearing a sweatshirt or something from a college in Sacramento."

The sweatshirt was from Sac State. Swede got it for me when I was in first grade, to remind me to do good in school because he expected me to go to college. It was big enough that I wore it the rest of grade school. Jimmy had it now. "It probably was us."

"That'll make your grandfather feel better about selling."

"So, you bought their house?"

"I bought the little house."

"The little house?"

"They'd kept it empty for years, hoping your mother would come back, but when I needed a place, they let me rent it. Then when they moved, they sold it off separate to me."

"Separate from what?"

"Why, the farm. Didn't your mother tell you about growing up on the farm?"

"My mother grew up with cows and pigs and chickens?"

"No." Maggie Hogan laughed. "Grapes. Eighty acres of them."

I didn't know they grew grapes in Pennsylvania; I thought it had to be hot. But two houses? They must be rich.

"Your grandfather wanted the place to stay in the family, but your mother was their only child and there wasn't anyone else. They bought a nice little place near the river in Sacramento, with fruit trees and all. Your grandmother sent me pictures."

"Do you have my grandparents' phone number, Ms. Hogan?"

"Yes, of course I do. But no one's there right now."

"Are they away on vacation?"

"Well, no. Not on vacation."

I waited for her to explain.

"Your grandfather's in the hospital. He fell and broke his hip."

My stomach sank. "What hospital?"

"UC Davis Medical Center."

Not that far from our apartment. "Won't my grandmother be at home part of the time?" I asked.

"I really need to talk to your mother."

"The truth is, she passed on a few days ago. That's why I was taking the kids to our grandparents."

"Oh, oh, heaven help us." She sounded a lot more upset than I expected. Maybe I shouldn't have said anything.

I tried to explain, "You see, there's no one else to take them."

"Oh, no."

She didn't think they'd want the kids.

Maybe they wanted to be near their daughter; that didn't mean they'd want anything to do with her mixed-blood children.

"I wasn't sure if they'd want me, but I figured they'd take Jimmy and Missy. Their daddy was white." There, I'd said it.

"Oh, Michael. Your grandma wanted you in her life, so much."

I heard the word and knew, but I asked anyway. "Wanted?"

"Cancer got her, last spring. She was sixty-seven."

About the time we were moving into the apartment.

"How old's my grandfather, then?"

"He was a bit older than Angelina."

"So he probably wouldn't take the kids even if he hadn't broken his hip, would he?" I could feel Maggie Hogan holding her breath. "And he never wanted me, did he?"

Silence can be so loud.

-43-

The ice crashed into the bucket. I reminded myself to take a breath, a deep one. The carpet on the floor was worn thin in the middle of the hallway. In front of the door, I took another breath, then went in and put the bucket down on the tray with the individually wrapped plastic cups.

"Shenia, what's your daddy's cell number?"

"I don't have it memorized."

"You have it written down in that little book you had out earlier?"

She crossed her arms and started to speak, "Michael..."

Before she could say anything more, I grabbed her pack and dumped it onto the nearest bed. She tried to get the book, but I snatched it up first and headed for the door.

"What are you doing?" she demanded.

Jimmy and Missy were staring at us now, frightened.

"I'm calling your father."

"Don't do that."

"Why, is there something else you haven't told me?"

"I got another email from him this morning. He was frantic about the weather. They told him we were spotted in Salt Lake. I told him they were wrong, we were nowhere near the snow."

"Am I still a suspect?"

"He didn't say anything about that and I didn't ask."

"A suspect of what?" asked Jimmy.

It was time to tell the kids.

"The police don't think Mama took those pills herself."

"Lester," whispered Missy.

Shenia cut her off. "Except no one's seen Lester anywhere near your place, and Michael was marked absent from one of his classes that day."

"They think you did it?" Jimmy yelled. "That's crazy."

"Yeah," I said. "They'll figure it out when they talk to the guidance counselor. I was with him at the beginning of a class, so the teacher marked me absent. That's not a problem. Shenia, I'm going to go call your father."

I spun on one foot and was out the door before she could say anything else. I should have put on my hat and coat. The manager was back at the desk and this was a private call. I felt my front pocket; the keys were there. I went out the lobby door and walked around the building to the car. I wrapped up in one of the blankets, put the driver's seat back as far as it would go, and settled in to make the call.

Just in case Shenia figured out where I was and came to try and stop me, I pushed the button to make sure all doors were locked. Her father's cell number was on the inside cover of the book. I was sure he'd have it on and ready to take a call from Shenia.

I punched each number and checked the screen to make sure I'd done it right. He thought I'd killed Mama, but there wasn't anyone else I could ask for help. I pushed send.

It rang three times before he picked up.

"Hello?"

"Mr. Brown?"

"Who is this?"

My voice froze. He hung up. I swallowed and pushed send again. As soon as it connected, I started talking.

"Mr. Brown, this is Michael McCarthy."

"Where's my daughter?" he demanded.

I had the right number. "She's in the motel room with the kids."

"You're staying in a motel with my daughter?"

I was glad he couldn't get his hands on me. "Girls on one bed, boys on the other, sir, and when you talk to the guidance counselor I know he'll remember talking to me. It was about a work program they've got where you can get paid and get school credit at the same time."

"If you're innocent, why did you run?"

He was talking slow now, maybe trying to keep me on long enough to trace the call. Could they do that with a prepaid phone? Probably. Didn't matter anyway.

"We didn't want to be split up. I was trying to take the kids to our grandparents."

"Why didn't you call them instead?"

"We've never met them, sir. There was a break when my mother and father hooked up."

"Then what makes you think they'll take you now?"

"I didn't expect them to take me, sir, but I thought they'd take the kids, 'cause they're little and cute and white, but I just found out our grandmother's passed and our grandfather's in the hospital and probably can't take the kids anyway, 'cause he's old and has a broken hip, and I don't know what to do now, sir. And you don't have to trace this call, 'cause I'll tell you, we're at the Super 8 in Laramie, Wyoming."

"Wyoming!"

I gulped a breath and kept going before he could say anything more. "We were headed to Pennsylvania, sir, and it was snowing and I nearly killed us all, going off the road, and the semis, but no one got hurt, and the car's okay, but I don't want to drive anymore and Shenia hasn't even tried driving on the snow and now our grandfather's at UC Davis right there in Sacramento, and we never even needed to come this way, and I'm sorry and I don't want anyone to get hurt." I paused but he must have been too stunned to say anything. "Could you please come get us back there safe and sound, sir? Please?"

"Your grandfather's at UC Davis Medical Center?"

"That's what I was told, sir."

"What's his name?"

"Michael Dolan."

"But you've never met him."

"No, sir. We found their old phone number and when I finally got a person this morning, the lady who has it told me about their moving to Sacramento and my grandmother dying and his being in the hospital."

"What's that phone number?"

I gave it to him, then asked, "Will you please come get us, sir?"

"If I fly out there, you're going to stay put at the Super 8?"

"Yes, sir."

"And you want me to drive you back here?"

"Yes, please, sir."

"Why not fly all of you here?"

"I thought of that, sir, but I don't think we'd have enough money to do that, or even take a bus, and it would leave the car sitting here, and that's all we've got now, and we might have to sell it to bury Mama, but I don't know how to do that and it's not in my name, so I probably couldn't anyway."

He interrupted my rambling. "Let me talk to Shenia."

"She's in the room, sir. I'm sitting out in the car with the doors locked 'cause she was a little upset that I was going to call you."

He chuckled. Maybe he wasn't going to kill me, after all. Maybe he was starting to believe I didn't hurt Mama.

"You tell her to answer that phone when I call you back. It'll be a few minutes. I'll need to call my captain, run this past him and make travel arrangements."

"Yes, sir."

I walked back to the room about a thousand pounds lighter.

-44-

"You didn't really call my father, did you?"

Shenia was standing by the desk, her arms crossed. Missy stared at me from the bed where she was huddled up with her eyes wide and scared. Jimmy moved over to put a hand on her shoulder.

"It's okay, Missy," he said. "Michael knows what he's doing."

"Tell me you didn't call my father," Shenia demanded.

"Everyone sit down and listen. It's okay," I reassured them. "Come on, sit down and relax, Shenia."

"Did you call my father?"

"Yes, and he's going to call you back in a few minutes."

"And you want me to relax?"

"I think he believes me. Even if he doesn't, they'll figure it out."

"What about getting the kids to your grandparents? What about that?" Shenia demanded.

"I got hold of that lady."

"Is our grandma black?" asked Missy.

"No, Missy," I said. "The woman on the phone was a friend of hers, and I'm pretty sure she's black, but I don't think our grandma was."

"Was?" asked Jimmy.

I nodded. "She's gone."

"What about our grandpa?" he asked.

"He's in the hospital with a broken hip."

"They made him stay in the hospital?" Jimmy asked. "They didn't make me stay when I broke my foot."

"He's old, Jimmy, real old," I explained. "When old people break their hips, it's bad. They don't heal the same way as a kid."

"You should go see him, anyway," said Shenia.

"We probably will," I said.

"My father's not going to let us drive on to Pennsylvania."

"No. I'm hoping he'll take us back to Sacramento." So I explained about the photo and how they sold the family farm to move and try to find Mama in California. "They put notices in the newspapers, but who reads those, anyway? And Mama was going by Johnson.

They didn't know about Swede; they were still looking for Lynn McCarthy."

"So how'd you leave things with my father?"

"I told him where we are and asked him to come and drive us back to Sacramento. He said he had to run it past his captain."

"He didn't sound angry?"

"Not when we were done talking. But make sure to tell him you've been cuddled up with Missy at night, not me."

The phone rang then and I handed it to Shenia. She turned away from us while she talked.

"Hello?" she said. "Yes, Daddy... We're okay. No one got hurt... Michael did real good... No, I won't... No, we haven't... It's not like that... We've got the kids with us, we've been taking care of them... This is the first time we've stopped in a motel. We slept in the car the other nights... We will."

I could tell when her mother got on the phone.

"I'm sorry... I know... I know... I will... Okay, I know... We will... I promise... Okay... I love you, too. Bye."

Shenia ended the call, then turned to look at us.

"Well," she said. "I am in big trouble with my mother for using her card as well as running away and making her cut short her visit with Auntie Char and worrying her sick."

"What about your father?" I asked.

"He'll be here about dinnertime. I can't believe it, but he agreed to drive us back. He said neither of us is to drive anywhere at all. We're to stay put. He'll get a taxi from the airport."

"So we're supposed to sit in this room all day?" Jimmy fussed.

"Yes," I said firmly. "No one goes anywhere. We've got plenty of food and you can watch TV."

"You better get rid of that Kansas plate, though," said Shenia. "I don't even want to have to explain that to my father."

"Good point. I'll put the old ones back on right now. Glad we didn't toss them."

"Lester's bad," said Missy. "He..."

"He won't be able to hurt you," I said.

I didn't want her to be scared.

Once Brown had made all the necessary arrangements, he went to update Schuster.

"The kid called me. They're in Laramie."

"They got that far? They must have driven through some hellish weather last night."

"He was pretty shaken up. Sounds like they had a close call of some kind, but he said no one got hurt and he wants me to come get them. So I guess you were right. He must be innocent."

"The guidance counselor just called and confirmed the kid was in school. But why were they in Wyoming?"

"They were afraid of being split up and headed to Pennsylvania thinking their only relatives were there."

"But?"

"I talked with a friend of the family back there, the one they ended up contacting. Their only surviving relation is the maternal grandfather. He's here in UC Davis with a broken hip. Sounds like he disowned the mother when she got involved with a black man. Faith is going to go talk to him at the hospital after she takes me to the airport."

"No offense, but I wouldn't want to be him. I mean, I like your wife, but I can imagine what that talk will be like."

"No offense taken."

"So, you're going to go get them?"

"I'm taking some personal time. I already had the weekend off."

"Must be nice," said Schuster. "I can't remember the last time I had two days off without getting called in on a case."

"Sometimes the uniform's not so bad."

"We'll want to interview them as soon as possible. Don't do it yourself, but make note of anything they say spontaneously."

"Okay."

"Have you called Social Services to line up care for them?"

"Faith is taking care of that, too."

-46-

We all settled in and watched a movie together, then made some lunch from the cooler.

"We should clean up," Shenia announced.

"I know I need a shower, but I'm a little scared of what your father will say," I replied.

"He'll get over it. The kids are here, after all."

"Can I have a bath?" Missy asked.

It was the first thing she'd said in hours.

"Sure, honey. We can make bubbles with my shampoo."

"You brought shampoo?" I asked.

"You didn't?" Shenia replied.

Shampoo and all that had been the last thing on my mind.

"You should shave," she said. "You're starting to look a little rough."

I didn't shave more than once a week yet, but I knew she was right. A smooth face would leave a better impression on her father.

"I didn't bring a razor," I admitted.

"I brought some disposables. You can use one of them and keep it. They're good for more than one shave."

Missy went first. When she was done, Shenia brought her out wrapped up in a big towel and sent Jimmy in next.

"Make sure you take your clothes in there," she told him. "You're not little like Missy."

He puffed up some at that, like he was already a teenager.

"And make sure you use soap and shampoo," she added. "You can use mine or the little motel ones."

He came out smelling like Shenia.

"I guess I'll go next, unless you want to," she said.

"Ladies first," I replied. I was not comfortable with this at all.

She took her pack into the bathroom and closed the door. I didn't hear the lock, but she knew none of us would walk in on her. At home, we'd multi-use the bathroom, because there was only one, but we had a curtain you couldn't see through and we were all family. The motel shower curtain was so thin you'd be able to see shapes, maybe more.

That thought, with Shenia in there and the water running, left me pulling a blanket over my lap so the kids wouldn't see what was happening. Jimmy knew about that stuff. Swede had asked me to sit in on that talk with him, so Jimmy would be comfortable asking me questions when his father was gone. I didn't want him to notice and tease me about it in front of Shenia, though—or worse, in front of her father.

Focusing on cartoons with the kids helped.

Shenia came out of the bathroom all dressed, but her skin was dewy and her hair was still damp. She shook it some to open up the curls and finger combed it right there in front of me.

I about died. She smelled so good.

"Your turn," she said.

"Okay."

She sat down with the kids. I got my stuff together, deliberately not looking her way. Once I was in the bathroom, I turned the lock as quietly as I could. Shenia may have been comfortable naked in here with an unlocked door, but I was afraid Jimmy or Missy might come in while I was in the shower, not thinking about how thin that curtain was, and I didn't want any of them to see me. The shower took longer than it should have, 'cause I started thinking of Shenia again and how I was here naked with her right in the next room, and that she'd been naked in this very shower right before me. I almost used her shampoo, but then I realized her father might notice I if I smelled like his daughter, and that might not be a good thing. In fact, thinking of that was like turning the water to straight cold. I used the little motel bottles.

The next couple hours, we took turns picking what to watch on TV. At least the kids and I did. Our old set didn't work with HD and we hadn't had cable for a long time, so watching television was a real treat for us. Shenia watched a little, but mostly she was on her computer.

"Jimmy, the way you're going through that food, it's a good thing we don't have to go all the way to Pennsylvania," she said when he made another sandwich so fat he couldn't get his mouth around it.

"He's growing. I was the same way when I was that age."

"Think I'll get as tall as you?" Jimmy asked.

"I'm not sure. My daddy was really tall, I think. Course I was tiny when he died, so maybe it just seemed that way, but I don't remember feeling as small around Swede."

"Do you think we'll be able to live with our grandpa?" he asked.

"It's not just his hip," I said. "He's really old and hasn't lived around kids in a long time."

Shenia caught my direction and added, "Sometimes, when an old person has been living alone, they don't want to have to get used to other people being around."

"How do you know he's been living alone?" asked Jimmy. "Maybe he has other grandkids, and he'd like more."

"Maggie Hogan said we're his only grandkids. Mama was an only child. And maybe he will want to see us and have us live with him, Jimmy, it's just maybe he won't, either. And I don't want you getting all excited about something and then not have it happen."

I motioned toward Missy. She'd hardly said a word all afternoon. She was taking Mama's death really hard. She didn't need any more hurt or disappointment. Jimmy got my silent message and quit arguing. It didn't make me feel better, though. Even if we got lucky and the old man took the little kids, the crippled old bigot wasn't going to want me. I got up and put on my jacket.

"We told my father we wouldn't go anywhere," Shenia objected.

"I'm just going to straighten up the car."

"Don't be out there too long," said Shenia. "It's freezing."

"I'll help," offered Jimmy.

I needed to get outside by myself for a while, but he needed to get out and move around.

"Put your hat and mittens on," I told him, as I put on my own.

Jimmy helped me fold up the blankets and pile them in the back. I left one side empty for our bags and the cooler. Then we cleaned out all the trash we'd accumulated.

"It'll be more crowded with an extra person in the car," I said.

"You sure he's not gonna arrest you?"

"Even if he does, I didn't do anything, so it'll work out okay."

"I'm not that dumb," said Jimmy. "I know things don't always turn out fair or right."

"There's lots of people who can say I was in school. It'll be okay."

The wind had died down and it seemed to be warming up some. It was still awfully cold, but it wasn't frigid anymore.

"You want to take a walk?" I asked.

"Yeah."

We went all the way down to Third Street, where there were a bunch of businesses.

"I didn't know they'd have Chinese restaurants in Wyoming," said Jimmy.

"Neither did I."

"Do you have the cell phone?" he asked.

"No. Shenia used it last."

"Think we should head back?"

"Probably."

As we walked back to the motel, the sun broke through the clouds low in the sky.

"Maybe it will be nicer tomorrow. That's what they were saying on the Weather Channel," said Jimmy.

"I hope so. In any case, I won't have to be driving. I may never drive again."

"You were always talking about getting your permit," he said.

"Yeah, I know. But I almost killed you guys."

"We just slid off the road."

"Jimmy, what if we *had* rolled? Someone would have been hurt."

He didn't have an answer.

"Whenever I used to hear about someone wrecking a car, I always thought it was 'cause they'd done something stupid," I told him. "Now maybe being out on that snowy road was stupid, but if it was, there were a whole lot of stupid people out there."

"It wasn't that bad," he said.

"I never saw it coming, Jimmy. One second everything was fine, the next we were sideways in the road. What if a semi had been coming up fast? Do you think they'd have been able to miss slamming into us?"

"Probably not," he admitted.

"Right."

"Well, you've got to drive sometime," he insisted.

"No I don't. It's bad for the environment, anyway."

-47-

Carmella opened the door for the detectives. Schuster and Martinez stepped into her tiny apartment.

Schuster wandered around, peeking into the kitchen, bedroom, and bath while Martinez did the talking. "Thanks for letting us in."

Her eyes followed Schuster. "You're not going to find anything, and you need to stop harassing my neighbors."

"We're not saying that you'd willingly hide your brother."

"You've got that right."

Schuster picked up the baby monitor from the end table and turned to Carmella. "Where's your baby?"

"With a friend. We watch each other's kids so we can do laundry and shop. If you two could hurry it up, please? I've got things to do."

"What if he threatened you?"

"He won't. Not after I got him locked up."

"Well, if he did, tell us now, while he's not around."

"I told you, he hasn't been here since he first got out. He stopped by once and I sent him packing."

"Lady down the hall thought she'd seen him when we showed her his picture. Thought he was living here."

"She's wrong. No one but me and my baby live here."

Schuster handed her a card.

"We need to talk to him. He's a suspect in a homicide."

"I haven't seen him and I don't expect to."

She held the door open until they finally left. She shut it, turned the deadbolt, then went over to the baby monitor and picked it up.

"Good enough for you? I got rid of them. Bring my baby back."

"Where did you go?" Shenia was steaming. "Don't tell me you just went out to the Explorer. I checked. Where did you go?"

"We took a walk down the road into town some. We needed to get some exercise before we get back into a car again."

"Me, mainly," said Jimmy, taking some of the heat for me. "I've never sat so much in my whole life."

"Well, you should have told us," said Shenia.

"What time is it?" I asked to change the subject.

"It's after four. My father's going to be here in less than an hour."

"Is he going to want to head back tonight?"

"I'm not sure; he didn't say."

"Well, we could sleep here. I paid for this room until tomorrow morning, but let's have everything ready to go in case he wants to leave right away."

We were packed and sitting on the beds—girls on one, boys on the other—when he knocked on the door. It was easy to tell it was him; he knocked like a cop. Shenia and I both popped up and she opened the door. He took in the room right away and he seemed to relax some, maybe because I looked ready to piss my pants.

"Have you eaten?" was the first thing he said.

"Not since lunch, except Jimmy," said Shenia. "He doesn't stop eating."

"We have food in the cooler, sir," I offered.

"Good thinking. Are you ready to go?" He was looking at me.

"Yes, sir. We need gas, though."

"Good," he said. "I checked road conditions with highway patrol. I'd like to get some miles behind us before we stop for the night. It's about fourteen hours of driving altogether."

"If nothing goes wrong," said Jimmy. "It took us about thirty-six hours to get here."

He'd turned off the TV and was standing beside me. I almost kicked him for correcting Mr. Brown, but Shenia's father didn't seem to take offense.

"That included sleeping time, too, didn't it?" he asked Jimmy.

Jimmy nodded. "Shenia drove the first night all the way to the Salt Flats, and we slept there some, then the next night it was snowing bad and we slept at another rest stop all night, then we came here this morning."

"How'd you keep warm at the rest stops?" Mr. Brown asked.

He was checking my story that Shenia and I hadn't cozied up, so I kept my mouth shut. Jimmy's answers satisfied him.

"Well," said Mr. Brown, "get your things. Michael, how did you pay for the room?"

"Cash, sir."

I'd never sir'd anyone this much in my life, but it kept sliding out of my mouth without even thinking about it. I pulled the rest of the cash out of my pocket and counted off what Shenia had gotten on her mother's ATM card.

"This is yours, sir. We didn't use any of it."

He looked a little surprised, but he took it.

"Check out and meet us at the car," he said.

"Yes, sir."

When I got to the car, they'd put the cooler in first, so it could be reached from the back seat. Everything else was behind it. That included a little duffle bag Mr. Brown had brought along. Shenia was sitting behind her father, Missy had the middle because her legs were the shortest, and Jimmy had the other side. They'd left the passenger seat for me.

I put my pack in with the rest, closed the back window, and took my seat. Mr. Brown drove straight to a truck stop.

"I'll go in and pay for it," I said.

"I'll put it on my credit card," he answered. "That money may have to last you awhile."

I got out of the car anyway, and checked the oil while he pumped the gas. It was down below the fill line, so I added one of the extras we had in back.

"You check the oil every time you gas up?" he asked.

"Yes, sir. It's been using some. Not much, but I've been keeping track of it for Mama."

"What year is the car?"

"Ninety-four."

"Well, that old it's entitled to burn a little oil. It seems to run pretty good."

"Yes, sir. Swede, that's the kids' daddy, he taught me how to do oil changes and everything else to keep it running good."

"Where is he now?"

"Skin cancer took him a year and a half ago. That's how we came to be living in those apartments, sir." I didn't want him to think we were trash. "I didn't hurt her."

"I know. The guidance counselor said you were in school."

"It was my fault we argued that last night." I glanced inside the car. They weren't paying any attention, but I still spoke quietly. "I didn't try out for basketball, so I'd be able to babysit after school when she got a new job, but she hadn't, and it was too late to get on the team."

"She was hired that morning."

"If I'd known that, we wouldn't have left town. I'd have found Lester by now." I probably shouldn't have told him that, especially as angry as it came out, but it was true.

"There's no sign of him. He was fired from his job several weeks ago, and the only address they had for him was yours."

"He hadn't been living with us since July."

"And none of your neighbors has seen him since then."

"Neither have I, but he might have killed our cat."

"When was that?"

"About a week ago. Mama told us Betsy had been hit by a car, but she got rid of the body before we got home. After that she was awful jumpy. I should have asked her about it."

"You know anyone who'd know if she kept seeing him?"

"She wouldn't do that."

Mr. Brown paused a minute and looked at me all sad. "She wouldn't let you know if she did, would she?"

He was right. I sighed. "I guess not. She knew how I felt. I never understood why she hooked up with him in the first place."

"She didn't have any close friends?"

"I can give you the names of our old neighbors, but Mama didn't stay in touch after we moved. She was shamed by where we were living." Then I caught myself. "Not that the neighborhood's all bad, sir, just the apartments."

"The neighborhood's terrible. It wasn't great when I was young, but it's really gone downhill since then. My wife's been trying to get me to move for ten years, but I'm reluctant to take on a mortgage when that place is paid for."

Our conversation left me less uncomfortable with Mr. Brown.

The first half hour on the road it was still light, so I could see that the sun had melted most of the snow and ice. The pavement was pretty much bare. But I was still nervous.

Once it was dark, I stared ahead, trying to tell whether shiny patches were ice or repair work on the road's surface. When a truck flew by us, Mr. Brown didn't slow down a bit.

He noticed my foot pressing into the floor, though. "You can stop driving, now, Michael."

"I'm just a little nervous with the semis."

He laughed. "A little? Did you drive after you went off the road?"

"Yes, sir, I got us to the motel."

"He drove about five miles an hour the whole way, Daddy," Shenia interjected.

"Thirty, and I got you to the motel safe and sound," I replied.

"Even though you weren't supposed to be driving at all," said Mr. Brown.

"I used to be counting the days until I could get my permit," I told him. "I don't think I want to drive now. If they won't let me get a permit, that's okay."

"Will they do that, Daddy?" asked Shenia. "Michael never drove on the road before this trip and he took over when it was icy because I was scared to drive and his stepfather had taught him how to handle a skid."

"That's not my decision to make," he answered.

We rode in silence awhile, and then he asked, "Can you find me some music that we'd all find tolerable?"

"That's not easy out here, sir, but I'll try."

-49-

Faith Brown stood with her arms crossed, glaring at the children's grandfather, who glared right back at her from his bed.

"Get out!" demanded Michael Dolan. He banged his fist on the metal meal tray in front of him, making a paper and pen fly off of it onto his blanket.

His roommate, on the bed nearer the window, glanced over, then went back to pretending to read the book he held.

Faith leaned forward. "You are the only adult left in their lives." She paused a moment for that to sink in. "If you don't get out of this place and take them in, they'll grow up in foster care."

"If you're so worried about it, you take them. Or are they the wrong color for you, too?"

"You are an impossible old bigot! At least sign that paper so they don't get separated before they can even bury their mother."

He glared at her again, but then he read the paper that had been on the tray. Finally, he signed it and shoved it at her. Mrs. Brown turned sharply and left before he could say another word.

"If I had grandkids, I'd be with them every moment I could," said the roommate.

"Don't you start in on me, too," grumbled Dolan.

-50-

Shenia made sandwiches for everyone. Her father ate his while he drove. Mama used to eat while she drove. Even Shenia had had coffee, but that was before I knew how easy it was to lose control. I was glad when he finished.

Maybe I could live somewhere I could walk every place.

Every so often, we'd lose reception and I'd have to find a new radio station, but aside from the music, it was pretty quiet in the car. Missy zonked out against Shenia, and then Jimmy fell asleep, probably out of boredom. Shenia dozed, too, but I was wide awake. I didn't see any more ice, but I was watching for deer or anything else that might come running out of the dark into the road. There had been enough excitement in my life for at least a year or two. I couldn't handle one more bad thing happening. Not right now.

We pulled into the same Flying J in Rock Springs for gas. That woke up everyone in the back seat and they all went inside while Mr. Brown and I took care of the car.

"We could sleep here at the truck stop," I suggested.

There was a parking area where you could see people snoozing in their cars, in spite of the temperature.

"I'm not tired yet. If we make it to Salt Lake City, it'll be an easy drive tomorrow."

"Will Shenia do some of the driving?"

"Oh, no. Shenia won't be driving for a long time to come. That's part of her consequence for this shenanigan. Go on in. I'll pull up by the store when the tank's full."

It was a relief not to have to stand next to him at a urinal. That would be too weird. When we all got into the car, he took his turn inside. He came out with a tall cup of coffee.

"You sure you don't want me to drive?" Shenia asked sweetly.

"You heard your mother," was all he said, and that was the end of that conversation.

When we finally pulled over at a motel near Salt Lake City, the kids had been asleep so long I was afraid they'd keep Mr. Brown awake. He must have had the same thought.

"I'm getting one room for Shenia and the children and one for you and me, Michael."

"You kids can stay up and watch TV, since you sleep so much in the car," I told them. "Just make sure it's appropriate, okay?"

"Don't worry," said Shenia. "I'm not ready to sleep, either."

I understood why I wasn't in with Shenia and the kids, but being alone in a room with Mr. Brown felt really strange.

"I'm going to take a long, hot shower," he said. "You done in the bathroom?"

"Yes, sir."

After he went into the bathroom, I took off my socks and shoes and the sweatshirt I was wearing, and then climbed into the bed closer to the outside door. I was sure I was too tense to sleep, but I never heard him get out of the shower.

Saturday: A New World

-51-

I woke up when he turned on the lights. He was already dressed and ready to head out.

"Good morning," he said. "Go ahead and take a shower. Just make it quick."

He was watching the Weather Channel.

If he noticed I was wearing my jeans and T-shirt, he didn't let on that it might be odd. I grabbed my bag and showered as fast as I could. When I came out of the bathroom I looked at the clock. It was 5:42!

"Shenia and the kids ready to go?" I asked doubtfully.

"I'm letting them sleep for now," he said. "You and I need to talk. Come on, I'll buy you breakfast."

There was a Denny's near the motel.

Mr. Brown ordered a steak breakfast and I ordered the Grand Slam, the cheapest breakfast on the menu. I didn't want to impose any more than we already were.

Whatever he wanted to talk about couldn't be good, or he'd say it in front of the kids. The waitress took our menus and left.

He cleared his throat and said, "Well, Michael."

He paused and I sat quiet, waiting.

"Well," he said, "You shouldn't drive without a license, and the trip was definitely a mistake, but I am impressed with how serious you're taking your responsibilities."

"I never want to drive again."

"That's what I mean. You're overreacting to your near miss, while most teens would brush it off. But that's not what we need to talk about."

He paused an awfully long time. What else could possibly be wrong? Finally he took a breath and continued.

"I talked with Shenia's mother after you fell asleep last night."

"And?"

"It's your grandfather. She went to talk to him."

"At the hospital?"

"He's not in there now. They moved him to a nursing facility."

"Does that mean he's there for good?"

"No, they say he should be able to go home eventually."

I was tired of pussyfooting around this. "He doesn't want us, does he?"

Mr. Brown gave a big sigh, like he was relieved not to have to figure out how to tell me. Then he said, "That's only his first response. He might change his mind."

"I doubt it," I replied.

"I'm sorry."

"It's not your fault. I knew it. When I was little and my daddy died, Mama called them. They would have let her come back, but they didn't want me."

"Maggie Hogan told me your grandmother didn't know what had transpired between your mother and grandfather, Michael. By the time she found out, your mother had disappeared."

"We moved to California with Swede."

"That's why her name was Johnson while yours is McCarthy?"

"Yes, sir."

"That's why they couldn't find her."

The waitress brought our orders and I started forcing the food down, since he'd bought it. My throat seemed to be working against me, though.

Mr. Brown ate like he'd been starving, but he still kept talking. "Your grandmother wanted to find you. That's why they moved."

"But she's gone." I stared at my plate.

"Right now your grandfather's not doing well. The doctor says it's more mental than physical, that the old man hasn't wanted to get better and go home to an empty house. The doctor thinks being needed might make the difference."

"He might want the little kids," I said with cautious hope. "I don't want to see them going into foster care, especially where I can't watch out for them. He would have liked *their* daddy."

"You might be right. Shenia's mother said ethnicity does seem to be an issue for him."

"That's an awfully nice way to say he's a bigot."

"Politically correct," he admitted. "I wanted to let you know before you see him."

"Thank you, but I already had it figured out."

"Anyway, we've decided the three of you can stay with us while you get to know him. Shenia can share her room with Missy and you boys can use her brother's bedroom. The Army's got him overseas now; he won't be using it."

"That's awfully kind of you, sir. Social Services will allow that?"

"Shenia's mother is working that out with them. She got written permission from your grandfather last night. As your only living relative, he's the one they look to, whether he likes it or not. They may have to inspect us, but when they can, they avoid placing kids—less expense and less paperwork."

"But when he gets out, if he still doesn't want us? Or if he doesn't get better?"

"We'll cross that bridge when we get to it."

We finished up and he called the prepaid phone and told Shenia to get the kids ready to go while we went for gas. Then we picked them up and checked out. He went through a drive-through to get them breakfast sandwiches, then we hit the road.

Mr. Brown wasn't much for stopping, and Missy wasn't fussing to pee every half hour, either. Finally, when we were seeing signs for gas in Elko, he asked if anyone needed a rest stop. Three voices rang out "yes" from the back.

"If we get gas here, we should be good until Reno," he said. "Don't dillydally."

I still took time to check the oil. It was down a quart again.

"Already?" Mr. Brown asked.

"It wasn't using it this fast before," I told him.

"We'll have to watch the idiot lights," he said. "How many quarts do you have left?"

"That was the last one. I'll get some more," I said.

While he finished putting gas into the car, I went in and paid for two more quarts of oil. We were beholden enough to Shenia's father. I didn't want him to think I was a leech.

Back on the road, I actually leaned up against the window and closed my eyes for a while. It wasn't icy anymore, it was daylight, and I was getting more comfortable with Mr. Brown's driving. I listened to the kids. Shenia had picked up some cards, and they were playing a version of go fish in the back, making up rules as they went along so it would work without a table.

Then Jimmy asked, "Where's Mama?"

Mr. Brown answered, "They had to take her to the coroner's office, to determine cause of death. She'll be there a few more days, and then they'll send her to a funeral home, wherever Michael tells them."

So I was still going to be in charge, even if we were staying with the Browns for now. I wasn't sure I wanted the responsibility of making arrangements for Mama, but there wasn't any choice. Who else would do it?

"Are Social Services going to split us up?" Jimmy asked.

"No," said Mr. Brown. "At least not right away. Until you see your grandfather and work things out, you're going to stay with us."

"Really?" Shenia sounded happy for the first time since I'd called her father.

"It's a temporary solution. You'll have to share your room with Missy, and the boys can stay in your brother's room."

"That's great!" said Shenia.

I was glad. I hadn't been sure how she'd feel about having all of us crowd into her space like that. It was different from helping us drive somewhere.

"Understand there will be no nonsense between you and Michael," her father warned.

"No, sir." I sat up straight.

"Of course not, Daddy," said Shenia.

"The rent on your apartment's paid through the end of the month," Mr. Brown said. "So we'll have a couple weeks to figure out what to do with all your furniture and things. Do you know if your mother had a will?"

"I think so," I said. "When Swede knew he was going to die, I think they both took care of that. He said he didn't have much left, he didn't want us to have to share it with the government."

"Good. He was right about that. Die without a will and they take a chunk right off the top. You'd be lucky if you didn't end up owing them money."

I didn't really care about the stuff, though. There wasn't much, and even if there'd been a million dollars, it wouldn't make up for losing Mama.

-52-

It's amazing how much you can sleep when life's throwing too much at you all at once. I guess everyone else ate stuff from the cooler while we drove, but mostly I leaned against the window and zoned out. I didn't even wake up when we stopped for gas in Reno.

We made it to the outer edge of Sacramento before the car died. Mr. Brown called AAA and Mrs. Brown. She got to us first and started by dressing down Shenia.

"You realize you are grounded, young lady?" She enunciated each word crisp and clear.

"Yes, Mother. I'm sorry for worrying you."

"And remember, you will not be doing any driving until further notice."

Shenia stayed all subdued and said, "Yes, ma'am."

"You children put your things in the back of my car," Mrs. Brown said in a polite, welcoming voice. After hearing her with Shenia, though, it was scary. "I'll take you to the house while Mr. Brown waits for the tow truck."

"I can wait with you, sir," I offered.

"That's a good idea," said Mrs. Brown. "I'll come back for the two of you while Shenia helps the children settle into their rooms."

Once they were gone, Mr. Brown said, "Her bark's worse than her bite, at least unless you cross her. Make sure you behave yourself with Shenia."

"Absolutely," I promised.

"I'll have them tow the car to the mechanic I usually use, unless you have one?"

"No, sir. Swede always did his own work, and I've been doing the maintenance."

"While you were sleeping, it drank four more quarts of oil."

"Four? It never used it that fast."

"It could be more to repair it than the car is worth," he said.

"I hope not. There's a lot of good memories in it." It was our last link to Swede.

"Well, we'll see what they say."

I made sure we took everything out of the car in case it couldn't be repaired. The tow truck was still there when Mrs. Brown came back for us. Her husband went straight for the passenger seat and I got into the back. She started in on me while she was driving. Her looking at me in the rearview mirror made me nervous. And she used the same tone with me that she had with Shenia.

"You do understand there will be no nonsense between you and our daughter while you are a guest in our home?"

"Yes, ma'am."

"You will follow our rules and you will not attempt to leave again."

"Yes, ma'am."

"You do realize that you could have been stranded in the middle of nowhere with that car, with those two little children?"

"Yes, ma'am."

As we pulled into their driveway, she asked Mr. Brown, "Did you explain everything to him?"

"Yes," he said.

"Michael," she said gently. "I am so sorry for your loss and that your grandfather is such a hard-hearted old fool. We can't change what happened to your mother, but I hope we can make him see the light. Meantime, you are welcome in our home."

"Thank you, ma'am."

"Now go on upstairs and put your things away while I get dinner on the table."

Shenia was in her room with Missy. Jimmy was in the room we were going to share.

He bounced over to a chest of drawers and pulled one open. "I left the top two for you. Mrs. Brown already put Antoine's stuff in boxes in the closet, so we could use this. Antoine's Shenia's brother. He's in the Army."

"Yeah, I know." I put my stuff on the bed. "You understand this isn't permanent, even if she emptied drawers for us to use. It's just not Mrs. Brown's way to live out of a backpack or boxes."

"I guess so."

"I know so. Three kids are more than anyone's going to want to take on, Jimmy. We're probably going to be split up eventually. If our grandmother had been alive, it might have been different, but she's not."

"You really think our grandfather won't take us?"

"He won't take me. He might take you and Missy if he was okay, but he's all crippled up now. So he probably won't."

"We could help him, especially you."

"Jimmy, I'm the reason we never knew our grandparents."

"Huh?"

"They pushed Mama away because of me, because my father was black."

"That's dumb."

"It's real, though."

"Well, it's dumb, and I'm going to tell him so."

"Don't do anything to make him mad, Jimmy. You and Missy would be better off with him than in foster care, and I wouldn't have to worry about you so much."

I could see he wasn't convinced, so I kept trying. "In foster care, they might not even let me know where you were living. They might not let me see you, or only on holidays or something. If we can get him to take you, at least I'll know where you are and even if we have to sneak around him, I could still see you some."

"Okay. I'll be polite when we meet him."

"Okay. Think of Missy if you want to get mouthy."

Shenia came to the door then and asked, "You all settled in?"

"We didn't have much to put away," Jimmy replied.

"We can go over to your place after dinner and get the rest of your clothes."

"Isn't it a crime scene?" I asked.

"Oh, yeah. Maybe not."

I heard a little bell ring.

"That's dinner," said Shenia. "My mother doesn't like yelling up the stairs, so she has a dinner bell."

We'd entered a new world.

-53-

There was a tablecloth on the table—not a plastic one, but a heavy white cloth. I was scared to death one of us would spill something on it. And there were candles on the table. At least they weren't lit. We wouldn't set the place on fire by knocking one over. I hadn't noticed the dining room being this fancy when we were here the day Mama died. I wondered if they did it up like this every night or if this was special for us. I'd have to ask Shenia later. It wouldn't be polite to say anything now.

Mrs. Brown told us all where to sit, girls on one side, boys on the other, with her and Mr. Brown at the ends of the table.

Then I remembered it had been round. They'd put a leaf in it for us. And the kitchen table was little. They probably didn't eat like this all the time. Or maybe they did. They had that little bell.

At least the kids took notice of the setting and waited to see how to behave without me saying anything. Mrs. Brown reached out her hands for grace. Mama wasn't much of one for religion, but we all had seen enough movies to know to take hands and wait for her to speak.

"Dear Lord," she began, "Thank you for the food we are about to eat. Thank you for bringing these children to our table safely. Let their mother rest in peace, Lord, and let her father see the light and take them into his heart. Amen."

We all echoed "Amen" and then Mr. Brown started serving up the plates, starting with Mrs. Brown. That seemed kind of silly, since it meant that everything had to be close up to his end of the table where he could reach it, but it was their way and they'd invited us into their home. Mama may not have said grace each night, but she'd taught us to be respectful of other people and polite. I didn't have to kick Jimmy once.

Shenia's mother turned out to be a good cook. When Shenia asked for the broccoli and then helped herself, I saw that was how it was done for seconds and I asked for the potatoes. When everyone had empty plates and no one was looking for more,

Shenia got up and started clearing the table. Jimmy popped up and started to help. I went to get up, but Mrs. Brown stopped me.

"More than two people clearing, and you'll run into each other. You and Missy can tidy up the kitchen when we're done."

I was puzzled. "When we're done, ma'am?"

"We haven't had dessert yet."

Shenia came back in with a pie and Jimmy had a half gallon bucket of ice cream.

"My wife makes the best pie you've ever eaten," said Mr. Brown.

He was right. As full as I was, that warm apple pie with ice cream on top was still one of the best things I'd ever tasted.

"Now," said Mrs. Brown when we were all done, "Missy and Michael may start the dishes while Shenia and Jimmy finish clearing."

I was surprised they didn't have a dishwasher, but it was an old house with a tiny kitchen. Maybe that was one of the reasons Mrs. Brown wanted to move. Someone who cooked as good as she did would probably like a big fancy kitchen with a dishwasher and all kinds of stuff for cooking.

I washed and rinsed. Missy dried. Shenia and Jimmy finished clearing the table, put food away, and took out the garbage. We made a pretty good team for our first time. When Shenia put dishes away, we all watched so we could help with that the next time.

"Does your mother always cook like this?" I asked.

"Whenever Daddy's home for dinner. The rest of the time, I usually put dinner together for whoever's getting home whenever."

"Really? Are you as good a cook as your mother?"

The idea was very attractive to me.

"I'm learning. I still can't make a pie crust as good as hers."

"Do you eat dessert every night?" asked Jimmy.

"No. No way. That was Mother's way of saying she was glad we got back safe."

"Oh." Jimmy heaved a big sigh.

Shenia and I both laughed. Then her mother came in to inspect the kitchen and we'd done good enough and she told us to come on back into the dining room to play a game.

The tablecloth and candles were gone, and Shenia's father was there setting up Monopoly.

"I don't know how to play that," said Missy.

"I'll help you," Shenia promised.

"We haven't been playing Monopoly since Antoine left," her mother explained. "It's not much fun with only three people."

"We usually play Scrabble without him," said Shenia.

"Do you play games every night?" asked Jimmy.

"Saturdays," said Mr. Brown. "Unless I have to work. I'm not sure what they do when I'm not here."

"We do something together," smiled Mrs. Brown. "I'm sure there were things you did with your mother."

I was glad she was busy setting up her money.

We did a lot of things as a family when Swede was alive, but Mama had been so depressed since then that we hadn't been doing much. And we'd never had a set night like this. We didn't even have any board games, just some cards. So this was one more new thing.

At least I had played Monopoly before, with friends. Jimmy seemed to know how to play, too, and Missy was little enough it didn't bother her to need help from Shenia.

With six of us, the game lasted hours. Missy almost fell asleep at the table, so I carried her up to bed. At the end it was Jimmy against Mr. Brown. The rest of us stayed right there at the table, taking sides, until they finally decided it was getting too late to keep playing. They counted up all their stuff and Jimmy was the winner. Mr. Brown told him he'd beat him the next time, but he wasn't mad.

Jimmy used the bathroom first, then Shenia, who took a lot longer than Jimmy, and finally me.

"We'll have to work out a schedule for school days," Shenia said. "That's what Antoine and I had to do."

"Your father said our staying here is temporary, and your mother said we won't be going to school for the next few days." At least not until we'd had a chance to bury Mama.

"Well, I have to be back in school Monday," said Shenia. She sounded kind of mad.

It *was* my fault she was in trouble with her parents.

Sunday: What!?

-54-

Michael Dolan stood between the parallel bars, panting.

"Two more steps," urged the pretty young therapist.

He kept most of his weight on his legs, using his hands on the bars more for balance than support. He grabbed her forearm to transition into his chair, though. His hand was pale against the brown of her skin.

"Great! That's the best you've done," she praised him. "There's no reason for you to still be in that wheelchair."

"Easy for you to say," he grumbled. But he softened the words with a smile.

"Your bones healed. You should have been walking out of here long ago. Why don't you want to go home?"

She'd asked before, but today he answered her.

"It's just a house. Angelina, bless her, made me sell our home. I was born in that living room; so was my father. Back then you were born and died at home. I spent my life taking care of it, building up the farm, thinking it would pass on to my daughter and her children."

"What about the rest of your family? Wasn't there anyone else to take over?"

"No. My only brother died young. Scarlet fever killed back then, no antibiotics, you know."

Family was more important to him than everyone thought. She put a hand on his shoulder. "The doctor said your grandchildren are coming to visit you."

"He told me, too. I don't have any say over my own life in this place," he complained.

"Well, then work harder and get out of here." Maybe she was wrong. Maybe he could be nice to her but not want a biracial child in his family. Some people were like that.

In any case, her job was to make him more independent and he was definitely trying harder than he had been.

"Rise and shine." Mr. Brown's voice boomed from the hallway.

It took a moment to wake up and absorb where we were and why, then I was up and pulling on my jeans. Mr. Brown was waiting when I opened the door.

"Good morning," he said. "I got permission for you to get your things right after breakfast. The detectives have to document what you take and they want to talk to each of you, too."

"They're working on Sunday morning?" I asked.

Mrs. Brown came by on her way downstairs. "Detectives work all the time. I don't miss that at all."

We ate quickly because the detectives were going to meet us at the apartment. At least Mama wasn't still there. It wouldn't be as hard going back now, at least for me. Missy didn't feel that way. When we all got up to leave, she dug in her heels and refused.

"No!"

I squatted down in front of her. "Missy, you need to get your things, and the policemen have to talk to you because you're the one who found Mama. They'll be nice to you."

"No." She was shaking.

"Honey, we'll all be with you," said Shenia.

"No. Lester will get me."

"Lester isn't there and I will be," said Mr. Brown.

"He'll know."

"Hold my hand," said Mr. Brown. "Even if he finds out, he'll know I'm protecting you and that he better leave you alone."

He held out his hand until Missy finally took it.

"Lester's bad," she said.

"Yes, he is," I said.

"He can't hurt you when you're with me," said Mr. Brown.

Missy locked onto his hand and they all started across the street.

I felt Mrs. Brown's hand on my arm, holding me back. "I'm concerned about Missy, Michael. She's acting like a much younger child. Is this normal for her?"

"No," I said. "Not at all. I figure it's having found Mama and all that. It started while we were on the road. I thought being here would make it better, but it's worse."

"Well, I'll make some calls and see if I can find a crisis counselor who works with young children."

"Thank you, ma'am."

One of the detectives was mostly bald and about Mr. Brown's age, the other one was obviously Hispanic and a lot younger. Once we were inside, Missy leaned against Mr. Brown, almost hiding behind him. They talked over her head, giving her time to get used to the strangers.

"This is Detectives Schuster and Martinez," Mr. Brown told us. Then he asked them, "Did you find a will, or the title to her car?"

"We already collected the will, for evidence," said Schuster. "It says everything goes to the kids equally. She also mentioned her parents as the only potential guardians."

"Good. Let Social Services know, would you? Their grandfather signed permission for them to stay with us for the time being."

"Was the title to the car with her will?" I asked.

"Yes," said Schuster.

"Was it still in Swede's name? We had to have it towed."

The detectives exchanged a glance.

Schuster answered my question. "It's in her name *or* yours, so the car belongs to you now."

No wonder I'd been a suspect.

When they took us up to get our things, Mama's door was closed and that was fine with me. Mrs. Brown had given us some empty boxes to load things up. School books, the rest of our clothes, stuff from the bathroom. Things we hadn't thought of or had room for when we took off. There was no point in getting everything, though, not until we knew where we were going to live.

Then Shenia, Jimmy, and I carried the boxes back to her house while the detectives talked to Missy first, since she'd found Mama. She still wouldn't let go of Mr. Brown.

I should have been glad she was looking to someone else like that, but part of me felt pushed aside.

-56-

"We wanted to walk her through it," said Schuster, "but I can see that's not going to happen."

Missy hadn't let go of Brown's hand at all or said a word. Even when they were packing their things, she'd just pointed and let Shenia pack for her. Now, with her brothers no longer there, she pressed against Brown even more tightly.

"Where would you like to talk, Missy?" asked Martinez.

She pulled Mr. Brown over to the couch. When he sat down, Missy surprised him by climbing up onto his lap and pulling his arm in front of her so she could still hold onto his hand. He brought his other hand up around her. She melted into him and pulled his arms tighter.

"You came home alone?" Martinez asked.

Missy nodded. She seemed more comfortable with the younger man, so Schuster sat back and took notes.

"Which way did you come in?"

"Front," she whispered.

"The front door?"

She nodded.

"Then what?"

"I went to the kitchen, looking for Mama."

Schuster could barely hear her.

"What did you see?" asked Martinez. "Was there spilled milk?"

"No. It was on the shelf with the other groceries."

"What did you do then?"

"I went to look for Mama."

"And you found her?"

"Not outside. The door was open, but she wasn't outside."

"The door was open?"

Missy nodded. "I slammed the door shut and locked it so he couldn't get in."

"So who couldn't get in?"

"Lester."

The men exchanged a startled glance.

"You saw Lester?" asked Mr. Brown.

Missy nodded. "He was in the bushes."

"You're sure who it was?"

"Yes. It was Lester. He was still there when we left. I know he came back to hurt Mama again."

"Again?"

"He killed Betsy and Mama made me promise not to tell the boys. Mama said he wouldn't come back anymore, but he did."

"Betsy?" asked Schuster.

"Their cat," Brown said. "Michael said their mother claimed it had been hit by a car. Missy, did you see Lester kill Betsy?"

She nodded and sniffed. "School got out early and Mama forgot to get me, so I walked home by myself. He was hurting her and I said I'd tell Michael and Lester killed Betsy and made us promise not to tell anyone or he'd come back and kill us, too."

"So when you saw him in the bushes, you locked the door?"

She nodded. "And I went upstairs to get Mama."

"And that's when you found her?" asked Martinez softly.

Tears were pouring down Missy's face now, but she was talking clearly. "Her neck wasn't like Betsy's, but I knew she was gone."

She took a big breath and sighed mightily. "I called Michael."

"Why didn't you tell Michael about Lester?" asked Brown.

"I did."

I was the last one they talked to. I had to explain why I hadn't listened better to Missy, but Shenia and Jimmy hadn't understood what she was telling us, either, which took off some of the heat. Of course, they also wanted to know why I didn't call 911.

"It was too late for an ambulance," I told them. "She was stiff and cold. Her note said to stay together, and I was afraid they'd take the kids away and I'd never see them again."

They didn't press me too much, probably because time of death had already been established so they knew I was telling the truth.

"What did your mother's key ring look like?" asked Martinez.

It wasn't the kind of thing you pay attention to, so I shut my eyes and tried to see them, and feel them.

"There was the car key, the apartment key, and there used to be a key to her office, but just the two after she was let go. It was one of those round metal rings, and she had a big plastic thing on it."

I opened my eyes.

"A key fob? What did it look like? Try to remember the details, Michael."

I closed my eyes again. I'd seen it a million times but without really looking at it. "It was oval, about an inch and a half by an inch. Swede got it for her when we were at Tahoe when I was little. It's a picture of the lake in winter, with a tree she said reminded her of home, bare branches. I think it says Lake Tahoe on the back, but I'm not sure."

I opened my eyes as a memory hit me. "And there's a little string on it—orange and yellow and red and brown. Missy made it for her—one of those things where she knots the strings together. She meant for it to be a bracelet, but she didn't start soon enough for Mama's birthday and gave it to her anyway. It's about so long." I held my fingers apart. "A couple inches, I guess."

"And you didn't go into the kitchen until you came back to the apartment for the keys?"

I nodded.

"Was the back door open or closed?"

"Closed."

"Was it locked?" asked Martinez.

"No. I don't think so. But when I left the second time, I made sure the downstairs windows were all locked, and the front door. Then I went out the back door and made sure I locked the handle and the deadbolt." I felt myself going through the motions again. "No, it wasn't locked before that."

"Any chance your mother's keys were in the outside of the lock?"

"No. I looked for them in case the spare car key didn't work."

"Could they have been in the car?"

"No. They weren't in the ignition and I emptied the car before it was towed. I'd have seen them then. I checked under seats and everything, in case they can't repair it."

"Was there any chance she'd been using the spare and put it away in the drawer?"

"No, sir. The spare still had the old apartment key on it. She changed the locks when Lester moved out."

-58-

Martinez watched Michael until he entered the Browns' house. Schuster was already reading over the interview notes.

"What do you think?" asked Martinez. "Missy says she locked the door and Michael says it wasn't locked when he went back."

"With the groceries still on the shelf? I think those keys were in the outside of the lock when Missy shut the door and I think the perp came after the girl. He was probably upstairs when Michael was looking for the keys."

"And he went out the back. Michael says he locked the door, but the neighbor says it was ajar. She might have been covering for entering the house, but in any case it wasn't locked anymore."

"We have to assume he knows Missy saw him."

"Probably," Martinez agreed. "Hopefully he saw them take off and thinks they're gone."

"We have to go back to his sister. She's our best bet," Schuster said. "We need to make sure Brown's aware, too. He'll need to keep close tabs on the kids, especially the little girl."

Shenia was upstairs with Missy. I could hear them talking.

Missy wasn't crying anymore. It was probably best for her to have a girl be with her, so I stayed downstairs.

I heard thumping and looked out the kitchen window. Jimmy and Mr. Brown were shooting hoops. There was a pole with a backboard and hoop in a patch of concrete next to the driveway. Activity was the best way for Jimmy to work out all his feelings.

I went into the living room and sat on the couch, staring at a flower arrangement on the coffee table. The flowers were color-coordinated with the furniture and the room. I could hear a shower running upstairs at the front of the house and figured it had to be Mrs. Brown in the master bathroom. Mama and Swede had their own bathroom in our old house.

Lester killed Betsy right in front of Missy because she walked in on him hurting Mama. Fortunately, Missy either didn't see exactly what he was doing to Mama, or she'd blocked it out of her memory. I wanted to kill him. Instead I sat there bawling as quiet as I could.

Mr. Brown came in and found me like that. I tried to stop, but when he pulled me up and put his arms around me, it felt like what Swede would have done and I lost it completely.

"Why did she let him come back?" I sobbed.

"We'll never know for sure, but it's clear she was afraid."

"It's my fault. She was afraid of what I'd do."

"No, Michael," said Mr. Brown. "She could have gone to the police. She *should* have gone to the police, but she didn't. You had no control over that. Do not blame yourself for her choices."

I brushed the tears off my face and backed away shaking my head. I knew it was my fault.

Mr. Brown stared down at those flowers on the table, then he started talking, his voice heavy. "Look, when Antoine was your age, the kids he grew up with started heading the wrong direction. I knew it and forbade him to be around them, but they were his friends, so he ignored me and I turned a blind eye. Then, on his eighteenth birthday, he got drunk and rode along in a stolen car."

"You're kidding," I said. "Did they get caught?"

He nodded. "They ran from the police and crashed. Antoine got away before he was seen. He came home and told me everything. He knew he'd messed up and was looking at a felony as an adult. I should have told him to turn himself in, but I didn't."

I was shocked. Mr. Brown didn't seem like that kind of cop.

He continued, "The kids who got caught covered for him, until one of them got busted for armed robbery."

He paused so long I knew I should say something, but I didn't know what. Then he started talking again.

"I was lucky to be busted back to a uniform and happy they reduced the charges to a misdemeanor and let him off on the diversion program. I paid his restitution. He's still trying to pay me back. That's why he went into the Army instead of college."

"Well, it's his debt," I said. "He should pay you back."

"Yes, but he shouldn't feel guilty about my demotion. That was the consequence of my own actions, not his. I hope someday he understands that's not his fault."

"Why did you cover for him?"

"I should have stopped him from hanging out with those boys."

"I don't mean to be rude, sir, but aren't you doing the same thing? Blaming yourself for his decision to ignore you and go along when they stole that car?"

"I guess I am, Michael. But that doesn't mean I should, and you shouldn't blame yourself for your mother's decisions."

He might be right, but I still felt like I should have done something.

After that, Mr. Brown let me be and went upstairs. I heard the shower stop and muffled voices overhead. Then the shower started up again and Mrs. Brown came downstairs.

All I wanted was some time alone, but it didn't look like that was going to happen.

"Michael, the girls are done in the bathroom. Go clean up and put on church clothes. I'll be sending Jimmy up right behind you."

"I know it's Sunday, but we don't have a church, ma'am."

"That doesn't matter. You can come with us to the late service. Then we'll have lunch before going to see your grandfather."

"Yes, ma'am."

As I headed up the stairs, I heard her mutter, "They'll need the strength of the Lord *and* food when they go see that old man."

Upstairs, Shenia already had Missy in her best dress. It was hard to believe how much better she looked already, now she'd turned over all her secrets to the grownups.

"You look really pretty," I told her. "Are you okay now?"

"Yeah, Mr. Brown will protect us." She headed down the stairs.

I turned to Shenia. "Jimmy and I don't have suits."

"That's okay. Let me help you pick out what to wear." She blew past us and looked through the dresser. She ended up picking out Jimmy's best cargo pants and a pair of dress slacks I'd inherited from Swede and grown into. But she wasn't happy with our button shirts. "These need a tumble in the dryer to get the wrinkles out."

By the time we were done in the bathroom and had our pants on, she was back with the shirts. She disappeared into her room while we put them on. Jimmy grimaced when I told him to tuck it in, but he did it and headed downstairs. As I started after him, Shenia came into the hall. She smelled different. Extra nice.

"You look good," she said.

The way she said it made me feel sexy, which made me feel very uncomfortable because we were in the hallway right outside her bedroom and the one I was using.

"Come on," she said. "We don't want to make Mother late for church. Trust me on that."

"Your mother's a little scary."

Shenia grinned and headed down the stairs.

With six of us, we had to go in two cars. Shenia and Missy went in her mother's little Subaru; Jimmy and I went in Mr. Brown's Expedition right behind them.

"Car as big as this, you'd think it would have more seat belts," he said. "I probably should have gotten the extra seat, but with two kids about to fly the coop, I didn't bother."

The few times I'd been to church, it had been one that Swede and Mama sometimes visited. Most of the people were white, and the whole thing was deadly dull. We sang a few songs out of a book and then sat and listened to the minister drone on about the lesson.

The church we went to that day was mostly black people, with lots of singing and halleluiahs and praise-the-Lords. For someone as formal as Shenia's mother, it seemed an odd way for her to worship, but she was joining right in with them.

She must have spoken to the pastor, too, because he asked everyone to pray for Mama and the little lambs she'd left behind. By the time we left, I *was* feeling better, and it looked like Jimmy and Missy were, too.

-60-

Lester's sister opened the door for Martinez and Schuster, but blocked their entry into her apartment.

"You already searched the place. You want to do that again, get a warrant," she said.

"Have you heard from Lester, Carmella?"

"At this point, I don't know if I'd tell you if I had."

"We have his prints, a witness who puts him at the scene, and we have a motive. Help us nail him. He won't get out as soon this time."

"Oh, you figured that out, huh? He did his full time, whoop-de-doo. Five years for what he did to me. Great system you have. He served most of it in county. That's like a vacation for him."

"So you'll tell us if you hear from him?"

"Sure—anything to get you to stop coming around here."

She took the card Schuster offered and closed the door. After a few minutes, she opened it to check the hallway. She then bolted the door and headed for her kitchen.

"They're gone. Give me the baby."

Lester dropped the child into her arms.

"I need to take care of their witness," he said.

"Why not leave?"

"You'd like that wouldn't you? Murder doesn't have a statute of limitations. You're going to help me take care of the witness."

"No."

She held the baby close and walked away from him.

"If I go down, I'll tell them you had me off that baby's father."

"That's a lie!" She faced him from across the room. "He was drunk and got mugged in an alley. I had nothing to do with it."

"So? If I get locked up for one murder, might as well make it two. And whether or not I'm caught, if you help them, I'll kill that baby. You know I will."

-61-

Mr. Brown treated us all to lunch at a small café. It looked fancier than a chain, but the prices were about the same as a Denny's, which made me feel better about all he was spending on us.

Mrs. Brown had a cup of herbal tea when she was done eating. She held it, warming her hands with the cup, like Mama used to do, staring into space. She turned that gaze on me a few moments, then took a sip of her tea. Finally, in a perky tone that I took as false, she said, "Well, when everyone's done, we'll go see your grandfather."

Missy and Jimmy hurried to finish up. I was already done.

"When did he break his hip?" asked Jimmy.

"Late August," she replied.

"That's more than two months," calculated Jimmy. He'd broken a couple bones himself and considered himself an expert. "A broken bone should be all better by now."

"Older people take longer to heal and their muscles atrophy, get weak, much faster than a young person's," Mrs. Brown explained. "Now wash up and make sure you look your best. You want to make a good first impression on your grandfather."

The nursing home was across town from the Medical Center and where we lived. It looked nice, with concrete pathways winding through gardens. But our grandfather was inside, and that smelled like a hospital, disinfectant with sickness hiding beneath it. Where we first walked in there was a small lobby like a doctor's waiting room, with a windowed office. Mrs. Brown pointed for us to sit while she went to the window.

"I've brought Mr. Dolan's grandchildren to see him," she said.

"Have a seat; I need to check his file to see if he's allowed visitors."

"His doctor knows we're coming."

"That should be in the file, please have a seat." The woman slid the window shut.

Mrs. Brown sat down with us, her mouth puckered tight.

We sat there a long time. The woman fiddled with a blue folder and made a phone call, then she disappeared for a while, then she came back and made another phone call. Finally she opened the window.

"The nurse will be out in a moment."

When she got there, the nurse said, "You weren't *all* planning to go in, were you?"

"My husband and daughter can wait out here," said Mrs. Brown. "But I'm going in with the children."

"You're the one he talked with Friday?" asked the nurse.

"Yes."

"Your husband is welcome to go in with the children."

Mrs. Brown started to argue, but Mr. Brown cut her off. "Faith, I'll go. Shenia, stay here with your mother."

As we walked down the hall, the nurse thanked him. They were walking ahead of us, but I could hear her anyway.

"They've been warned he's not enthused, haven't they?"

"I'm glad he's giving it a try," said Mr. Brown.

Jimmy glanced up at me, then he stopped at a drinking fountain with Missy, so she wouldn't hear anything else. I did, though.

"Actually, the doctor insisted. We know the situation with these children, but the doctor's concern is for his patient. He's hoping the visit helps Mr. Dolan."

"How serious is his condition?"

"His bone healed, but he's shown no interest in getting out of the wheelchair. His wife died a few months before he fell and he's been ready to die here. And if nothing changes, that's exactly what will happen."

Now, that left me with a world of conflicting emotions. Part of me wanted to say good riddance to the old man who'd shoved me and my mother out of his life; part of me wanted to play hero and save the day, since I hadn't done such a good job saving Mama; part of me wanted to curl up in a corner and cry because nothing ever went right for us.

Bottom line: I had to do what was best for the kids, and getting this old man to let them come live with him was better than foster care. It would be nice to think the Browns would keep all of us, but

I'd heard that word 'temporary' and I understood that's what they meant.

Mr. Brown waited in the hallway while the nurse took us into the old man's room.

He was slouched in a wheelchair watching television.

There were two beds in the room. There was stuff on the table by our grandfather's rumpled bed. The other side was empty, the bed stripped to the mattress cover.

Our grandfather was staring at the television, deliberately not looking at us, his face a picture of anger. I recognized his nose. There was one just like it on my face. Aside from that, he was a stranger.

"I told you I didn't want any more visitors," he grumbled.

"And the doctor told you we were disregarding that desire in your best interests. Now say hello to your grandchildren."

"Hello," he spat out, never taking his eyes off the television.

"Are you really our grandpa?" asked Missy.

He slipped up and glanced at her. Something soft passed across his face, then it was gone. "That's what they tell me."

Missy's face puckered up. "You don't sound like a grandpa."

His mouth worked some like he was trying not to cry. He looked at her again, longer this time. "You look like your mother when she was a little girl."

"Really? We never had any pictures from when Mama was little, but she said that I looked like her."

"Really. You do." He blinked a couple times, then looked at Jimmy. "You look a lot like my brother. He died young."

"I look like my dad, mostly," said Jimmy.

He handed the old man an 8x10 picture. His last summer, Swede had bought one of those disposable waterproof cameras and he'd asked strangers to take photos of all of us together when we were having fun on the river. Mama'd liked that one snapshot so much, she'd had it enlarged to hang on the wall.

When Lester moved in, Jimmy had hidden it in our room.

"That's your dad?"

"Yes, sir. You'd have liked him," said Jimmy. He set the picture on the bedside table. "You can keep it for now, while you're in here."

"What happened to him?" the old man asked.

"Cancer got him, summer before last," I answered.

The old man looked at me then.

"He wasn't your father," he sneered.

I knew Swede would have told him different, but that wouldn't have the same weight coming from me, so I just said, "He was a good father to all of us."

"Now my daughter's dead, you want me to take care of you."

He was glaring at me.

"The kids need you," I said evenly. "But you don't need to do anything for me."

"Humph," he snorted.

It was getting hard to hold back, and the nurse hadn't told us to get out because we were upsetting the old bigot. So, keeping my voice steady and calm I said, "But I hear you can't even take care of *yourself* enough to go home."

"My home's long gone," he snapped. "I'll leave here the same way Jones over there did." He gestured toward the empty bed.

"Where do you live?" asked Missy.

She was stopping an argument. She always did that. Mama called her the little peacemaker.

"Near the river."

"What's it like?"

"It's a piece of crap built in the seventies with a dinky piece of yard surrounded by other people."

"Mrs. Hogan said you've got some fruit trees?" I asked.

"Half a dozen," he spat out. "That place cost as much as we got for a hundred acres and two houses. Your grandmother was so sure she'd find Lynnie."

He sounded desolate and he seemed to drift off mentally. I wasn't sure if he was sad about losing his family's farm, or about moving and not finding my mother, or about losing his wife, or because he was never going to see his daughter again. At least he had feeling for something, whichever it was.

"We're sorry for your loss, sir," I told him, in a much kinder voice than I'd been using.

"I lost my daughter sixteen years ago," he snapped. "Now she's gone for good."

Missy teared up and sniffled, "We lost Mama Wednesday."

"I'm sorry about your mother," the old man said to her.

Then he turned to the nurse and snarled, "Get these kids out of here. I'm too tired to deal with this crap."

"Come along," said the nurse.

She whisked us down the hall with Mr. Brown. Once we were away from the old man's room, she said, "Well done, Michael. I think you challenged him just enough. We'll have to see if it carries over into his therapy sessions."

"What kind of therapy?" I asked.

"Physical therapy for his mobility, primarily, but he's also talking to a grief counselor."

"How'd he break his hip?" asked Jimmy. "Hips don't break easy."

"They can when you get old and your bones become more fragile," said the nurse. "But that's not why your grandfather's broke."

"What happened?" asked Jimmy.

"He was cleaning the gutters of his house and fell off the ladder. Apparently it was an extension ladder and it wasn't latched properly. It slipped and he fell from several yards up. Then his condition was further deteriorated by the fact that no one found him until the next day. It was lucky he didn't go into pneumonia."

"No one found him?" I asked. "He said he's surrounded by houses."

"He's on a cul-de-sac, that's what his file says. Apparently his neighbors were at work when he fell and probably they were inside all evening. A delivery man found him. He had instructions to deliver a package next door by putting it on their back patio."

"That's sad," said Jimmy, "to be that alone."

It was, but I wasn't ready to feel sorry for the old bigot.

"Thank you for taking the children in to see him," said Mr. Brown. "When will they be able to visit again?"

"They can come anytime, eight until eight."

When we got to the lobby, I hung back while the kids rushed to tell Shenia and her mother everything.

"What happened to his roommate Jones?" I asked the nurse.

I was pretty sure I knew the answer, but I wanted to be positive.

"He passed away last night. Fell asleep and never woke up. Heart failure. It was a real shock to all of us. But your grandfather will have a new roommate later today."

She made it sound like old people were disposable items that could be easily replaced. I left them and went over to join the kids and Shenia.

Mr. Brown followed a minute or so later and asked his wife to take all of us back to their house.

"I'll be there in a little bit," he promised.

"Mr. Dolan, I'm Sam Brown. Your grandchildren are staying with me. You've met my wife."

Dolan focused on the television as he growled, "My condolences. That's one pushy woman."

Brown laughed. "That's why you wouldn't let her come in today?"

The old man curled up one side of his mouth and glanced at Brown. "She's annoying."

"She can be, but don't quote me. Thanks for signing that release anyway. The children need each other right now and we're happy to help them until permanent arrangements can be made."

Dolan switched off the television and turned to Brown. "So what do you want?"

"Well, first of all, Michael's been holding up amazingly well, but the coroner's ready to release your daughter's remains, and he's going to need help making all the arrangements. We thought you might want to do some of that. Do you have a pastor you'd like us to contact?"

"Angelina was the churchgoer. Don't the children have one?"

"Apparently they've never attended church regularly."

The old man drooped. "Lynnie was brought up better than that. She should have had them in Sunday school."

"Our pastor could come make arrangements with you."

"That boy is not going to like my stepping in that way."

"He's had a lot thrown at him. He could use the help."

The old man looked at the picture Jimmy had left. "You seem to like the kid."

"He's got a level head and takes responsibility seriously. He was smart enough and had enough guts to call me for help when he was in a Wyoming motel with my daughter, even though he knew I was a cop and we were looking for him as a person of interest."

"What?" Dolan sat up straight.

Brown waved his hands in denial. "There was some confusion at first—he was marked absent—but that's been cleared up. We know who did it now."

"Have you caught the guy?"

"I'm not on the case, but they're having trouble finding him."

"Do they have enough evidence to nail the s.o.b.?"

"It's circumstantial, but strong. Missy saw him outside when she got home, before she went up and found their mother."

"Jesus, she found Lynnie?"

Brown nodded.

"All by herself?"

"Michael was across the street. He came as soon as she called."

The old man's voice cracked as he asked, "Will she have to testify?"

"Without her, the case is weak."

"Is she safe?"

"We've been keeping the kids together with us all day. I'm not sure how we'll take care of it tomorrow. My wife and I both work. Shenia will go to school, but I don't expect your grandkids to do that until after the funeral."

"What about police protection?" Dolan demanded.

"That doesn't happen in real life. It's not in the budget." Brown shrugged in disgust.

"How about my house? He won't know to look for her there."

"That would be good during the day, but at night I'd rather they were with us."

"The place is a mess, but there's cable. That should keep them busy. Maybe they could take care of my bird feeders." Dolan's energy picked up. "The seed's in the garage. And there's a stray cat I was feeding that's probably eating the birds now. The cat food's in the garage, too."

"I can take them over before I go to work in the morning."

"Could you bring me my mail and bankbooks? I need to balance my account."

"You didn't have anyone stop your mail or pay your bills?"

The old man shrugged his shoulders. "The bills come out of checking automatically. Angelina set that up when she was sick; she didn't trust me to keep track. She always did our accounting. But I should move money into checking to keep the balance high enough."

"I'll need a key."

"They're in the office here, locked up with everyone's valuables."

"Okay. Where will I find your bankbooks?"

"In the side drawer of the captain's desk when you first walk into the house. It's an antique piece with a slant lid. It was my uncle's." He switched from nostalgic to gruff. "I've got all my financial crap in that desk. Just get the books and don't poke around the rest of it."

Mr. Brown straightened away from the old man. "Make a list of what needs to be done at the house while I get your keys. It'll be good for the kids to keep busy."

-63-

On the way home, Mrs. Brown stopped to pick up something at the pharmacy and insisted we all go in with her. Until they caught Lester, it made sense, but it was also tiresome to have no time alone all day when that's what I needed more than anything.

She didn't make us stay by her in the store, but she told me to keep an eye on Missy and Jimmy while they wandered around. It was one of those places with a little of everything. Missy spotted a baseball hat that said 'Proud Grandpa' on it. I tried to get her to put it back, but she showed it to Mrs. Brown and they bought it.

"I have a nice gift bag for it at home, and you can make a card," she told Missy.

I wasn't sure he was even going to let us visit him again, so I was floored when we got back to the house and Mr. Brown broke the news that we'd be going to the old man's house the next day. "And Faith, he'd like you to call our pastor and the funeral home director to meet with him and Michael about the arrangements."

I'd hoped Mrs. Brown would take over the details of the funeral and all that, but I didn't know how I felt about the old man who'd disowned Mama doing it. I wasn't being given any choice in the matter, though, that was clear. I slipped out the front door to take a walk. Lester wasn't going to bother me. I wished he would, at least until Shenia caught up to me.

"Here, I brought you your hat," she said.

"Hardly need it, after Wyoming." But I put it on anyway.

She grabbed hold of my hand and we walked side by side. I walked fast, not thinking. She kept up with me until somewhere in the third block. Then she quit but held on and yanked me to a halt like an anchor. "Stop, Michael. Your legs are longer than mine."

"Sorry," I said.

"We shouldn't go so far, anyway."

We were in a stretch the streetlights didn't reach much, but I could still see her face, looking up at me so sweet. I pulled her into my arms and we kissed, real time-losing kissing. It was a good thing we were out there and not somewhere we could take it any farther.

-64-

"I saw the kid and his girlfriend and followed them back to her house. Her dad's a cop," Lester complained to his sister. "I didn't see the younger kids, but I'll bet they're there. He didn't come back out and her parents' cars were in the drive."

"All the more reason you should leave."

"You really want to get rid of me, don't you?"

Carmella kept her mouth shut. She and the baby were the closest targets if she antagonized him. He hadn't done anything to the baby yet. She wondered if he really had been the one that killed her child's father. If Tommy had been sober, Lester would never have had a chance, and he wouldn't be running her life again.

"You're going to watch the place for me tomorrow," he said. "You'll let me know when I can get at the girl."

"A little kid's testimony won't hold up. Why bother with her?"

"You'll do it."

He could at least have pretended to offer her a carrot, to tell her he'd leave her alone once she helped him. But he didn't need to. She'd been foolish enough to go against him once, and she'd been paying for it ever since he got out of prison.

Monday: More Surprises

-65-

"Sorry for getting you up so early," Mr. Brown apologized. "Shenia's mother takes her to school before going downtown to work. That's at rush hour. Your grandfather's house is in the opposite direction. It's not that far for me and there aren't as many people on the road when I go to work."

"That's okay," I mumbled.

It was still dark outside. The kids looked as sleepy as I felt.

Mr. Brown opened the back so I could put the cooler into the car. Mrs. Brown had packed a day's worth of food for us. He gave it an extra shove, then closed the back.

"I'll pick you up about four and take you to your grandfather. The pastor will meet us there so you can work everything out."

"Now he cares about her," I grumbled. "If he'd let us into his life when my father died, she'd still be alive."

"Maybe. But where would Jimmy and Missy be then?"

Mr. Brown gave me a moment to think that through. They wouldn't exist if we'd gone to live with Mama's parents, and I'd never have had Swede for a father.

"You can't change the past, Michael. Neither can he. Let him take some of the responsibility off your shoulders."

"Okay."

"On the other hand, here's a list of things he'd like you to do."

"You're kidding." I took the piece of paper he was holding out.

"No. I'm taking it as a good sign he's showing some concern for his home and that he's reaching out to you for help with it. The house has been sitting empty for two months. The mail wasn't even discontinued."

"So he's letting us go to his house because we'll do a bunch of work for him?"

"Mainly because it's safer for you to be far away from here."

"Safer?"

"For Missy," he said quietly. "She's a witness."

Witness. My stomach turned into a cold lump. I hadn't even thought about it that way. If Lester knew she saw him...

"I charged your phone last night," he said. "You have it?"

"Yes, sir."

"Good. Keep it on you and keep the children with you all day."

As I got into the car, I looked at Missy in the back seat, leaned up against the window, more asleep than awake. While we drove the early morning streets in silence, I put Mr. Brown's numbers on speed dial. I wasn't sleepy at all anymore.

Finally he turned off the main street into a pretty residential area. The homes looked older, but the yards and the houses were tidy and well kept. I didn't see a single window with bars on it.

"This is one of the areas Shenia's mother likes," said Mr. Brown.

The old man's house was on a cul-de-sac with three other houses. There was an old pickup in the driveway, the kind with rounded fenders, but it had a good paint job and the whole neighborhood looked pretty, except for his grass being too long.

Mr. Brown grabbed the cooler and handed me an empty box for mail. The mailbox was stuffed full, including a note from the mailman saying the rest would have to be picked up. Mr. Brown had already stepped into the house when I got to the door.

The place didn't smell bad, but it was a little musty from being shut up, and it was a mess. It was one of those places where all the rooms are open onto each other, so we got to see it all at once. There were piles of papers and opened mail and magazines all over, and coffee cups here and there, and takeout bags and boxes.

There were clothes slung over a chair at the dining room table, and every counter in the kitchen area was loaded. It looked like every dish and pan was dirty.

"Jimmy, there are some more empty boxes in the back of my truck," said Mr. Brown. "Go get them. You should put all the mail you find into this one so we can take it to him tonight. You can use the others if you finish the list and start sorting through things for him. He'll never be able to maneuver a wheelchair or walker in here the way it is, that's for sure."

He left as Jimmy came back with the boxes. "I'll see you at four."

"This place is a mess," said Missy.

"No wonder he doesn't want to come home," Jimmy said.

I waved the list. "Well, let's start with this, then maybe we can pick up some for him. We're supposed to fill the birdfeeder. The birdseed's in the garage."

The garage was attached to the house and it was tidy!

There was an Escort with a cover over it, a tool bench with a pegboard where each tool was outlined and hung in the proper place, some cupboards with index cards that listed what was in each one, and the birdseed right where he'd said it would be, in one of the cupboards that had birdseed and cat food on its card.

There was a small bathroom with a stall shower and more clothes hanging on hooks. It needed a good scrubbing.

We went out the side door. Missy and Jimmy ran ahead of me, around and behind the house. I hurried to keep them in sight.

There was a solid board fence from the garage to the edge of the property, then along the perimeter. There was a gate at the section that crossed to the garage, but we couldn't be seen from the street. The kids came running back from the far side of the yard.

"This is cool!" said Jimmy. "It wraps around both sides of the house, and there's a bunch of fruit trees, and he's got them labeled!"

"And there's a garden, with squash like Mama always made for Thanksgiving," said Missy. "Some tomatoes, too, but they're rotten and the plants are brown."

We'd had enough cold nights to kill the tomato plants, but for them to have lived long enough to drop tomatoes, he must have an automatic watering system.

"There's a fountain on the other side," said Jimmy.

"It's in a rose garden," said Missy. "I think. There's no flowers but there's a bunch of bushes with big prickers on them."

"And there's a deck with a door into the kitchen. It's set up so you can eat outside," said Jimmy.

I followed them around and spotted some drip line in the flower beds and garden area. There were plenty of weeds, too. I checked the list. It said to mow and watch for sprinklers along the edges. When I knew where to look I could spot them.

The ladder he'd fallen off was lying in two pieces behind the house. Putting it back in the garage was one of the items on his list, so Jimmy and I did that first thing while Missy looked for the kitty dish in the yard. The ladder hooks were labeled, too, so I knew we were putting it in the right place.

We filled the birdfeeders and put food out for the stray cat, though after this long it had probably moved on.

The grass was so thick I'd have to take the safety off the mower or it would clog up. We'd have to rake, and I wanted the kids inside while I mowed. We ate some breakfast out of the cooler. Jimmy turned on the television. The old man had cable and it hadn't been turned off. They found cartoons and were instantly glued to it.

I still asked, "Can you stay out of trouble in the house?"

"We won't break anything."

"If you tidy up, make sure you don't throw away anything he might want, like mail or old magazines."

"Okay."

I figured they wouldn't do anything until I went back inside and made them.

Swede had taught me how to use a gas mower years ago, so it was a cinch to get the old man's machine going. It was a big yard, the way the back curved around both sides of the house, and there were two patches of lawn out front that I mowed, too.

I decided to do the raking myself. I needed to be alone some. So it was almost time for lunch when I went back into the house. They hadn't picked up at all, but the television was playing to an empty room.

I hadn't told them to keep the front door locked.

My stomach knotted up.

"Jimmy! Missy!" I hollered from the front doorway.

I'd finished up out front. If they were gone, they had to have been gone at least an hour. I should have locked the front door when we first got to the house.

"Missy! Jimmy!" I hollered again.

"Up here!" Jimmy's voice came from inside the house.

They'd gone upstairs! I shut the door, locked it, and took the steps two at a time, shouting on my way. "You shouldn't be up here! He didn't tell us to do anything upstairs."

"You've got to see this!"

I followed his voice into a room decorated for a boy his age.

Everything was the way my grandmother had left it. It had to have been her. She'd fixed it up for me, when they came looking for us. I couldn't breathe.

Jimmy was sitting on one of the antique twin beds. "It's all ready for us. There's a room for Missy, too."

"They didn't know about you and Missy."

He ignored me. "Grandpa said I look like his brother that died young. I bet these were their beds."

"Probably."

This room was for me, though. I knew it.

There was a bin of sports equipment in a corner of the room, some of it looking like it had never been used. Jimmy pulled out a big old wooden baseball bat. I could tell it was heavy from the way he lifted it.

"Louisville Slugger," he read.

"I think that's a good bat from back in the day," I said.

"Cool."

"Where's Missy?"

He dragged me across the hall. This room had light pink walls and one of those wallpaper borders at the top with roses on it. The four-poster double bed was covered in a spread with roses all over it, and there were a bunch of pillows, all frilly and flowery.

There was an antique dresser with a big mirror in the middle and a space to sit there in front of it and a chest of drawers. All the furniture was matching wood with fancy carving on it. I figured they were family antiques. It had probably all been our mother's when she was growing up. Nothing looked new.

"Don't break anything," I warned Jimmy.

Missy was in the walk-in closet. There was a window with a seat under it that was the cushioned lid of a wooden box with old toys in it. Missy had it propped open and was playing quietly with some little dolls.

"Think those were Mama's?" asked Jimmy.

"I guess."

The window looked over the rose garden.

"We really shouldn't be up here," I told them. "He might not like it. Put the toys back, Missy. Make sure you leave things the way they were. We don't want him to think we're a bunch of snoops."

She grumbled, but started putting things back carefully. I figured I better stay and make sure everything looked okay, but I told Jimmy to head on downstairs.

Instead, he tilted his head for me to go out into the hallway with him. "There's something else you've got to see first. Remember how Mama gave away Dad's things right away? Remember she said that was the best thing to do?"

"Except the flannel shirt she wore sometimes when she was curled up reading, Jimmy. She made sure we all have something from him."

"Yeah, but it looks like Grandpa's kept *everything* the way it was when our grandma died."

"What do you mean? That was months before he got hurt."

"Come on, look."

He dragged me down the hall.

I glanced in the bathroom as we passed. It looked like it had been cleaned good, then left unused, just a little dust on things.

Jimmy was right about our grandparents' bedroom. There was still perfume and everything on a dresser similar to the one in the rose room, and clothes for both of them were in the walk-in closet. The bed was neatly made. Nothing was out of place.

"There's no trash up here at all," Jimmy said. "You think he's been living downstairs?"

"Probably. Looks like he hasn't been up here in months. He probably hasn't cleaned since she passed."

"That's not good, is it?"

"No, but he didn't expect us to be up here. So don't say anything to him about it."

"Okay."

We got Missy and went back downstairs.

I made them promise they wouldn't say anything to anyone about those rooms so the old man wouldn't get mad at us for snooping. I hoped they'd remember.

-67-

The baby started crying again. She didn't have enough bottles to sit here all day and watch this house. Carmella called Lester.

"You must have told me the wrong place."

"No, you saw the woman and the girl leave in the Subaru."

"But there hasn't been a sign of life since then."

"The Expedition was gone before you got there?"

"The Subaru was the only car here at seven this morning."

"He must have taken them somewhere."

"That's what I've been telling you. They're not here."

"Go park by the elementary school. Watch for the girl when they come out."

"I've never seen her; how would I know which one she was?"

"Yeah, stay where you are."

"Lester, a woman doesn't sit in a car all day with a baby on a street like this. They'll come around to see if I'm living in the car, and when they run the plates, those cops will be back at my door with a warrant this time."

"Fine. You win. Come on home. I'll be waiting for you."

Carmella looked at her gas gauge, looked at the crying baby, and then dug in her glove box. She pulled out a card and punched the number on it into her cell.

"I need a safe house? Do I have to use my real name or anything? Can I bring my baby?"

She listened a few moments.

"Good. I can make it to San Francisco. I don't want anyone to know where I'm from, no one."

As she pulled away from the curb, she told the baby, "We'll go back one more time, but when he leaves, I'm packing our things and we're getting out. This time, no one's going to talk me into pressing charges, either. He's *never* going to find us."

-68-

Mr. Brown picked us up at four and took us straight to the nursing home. The old man was dressed and waiting in his wheelchair in the recreation room. Missy ran right up to him and gave him a hug and a kiss on his cheek, as if he'd always been her grandpa.

She was so sure he was going to get better and have us come live with him, but she did good not mentioning going upstairs. "We didn't see your cat, but we put food out for her, Grandpa."

"She may be hiding with kittens somewhere. She looked ready to pop when I got hurt."

"We brought your mail," said Jimmy. "We put it in your room."

"I'll go through that later tonight. I don't sleep anymore."

"Your new roommate?" asked Mr. Brown.

"Never heard anything like it. Snoring is an inadequate term for the noise he makes."

"We got you a present," said Missy.

"You did?" He was a gentle old man with her.

"For when you go home, you'll need it. But I can't say anything else or it'll ruin the surprise. We're going to give it to you for Christmas. That's weeks and weeks away."

"We tidied up some so you can get around your house when you go home," said Jimmy.

"You didn't throw anything away, did you?" He seemed upset.

"No," I said. "Just some spoiled food, and the takeout containers. Anything you might want to keep, we put into boxes so you can sort through it but still get around your place."

The pastor arrived while we were talking. Mr. Brown introduced the men and left with Jimmy and Missy. It felt weird, knowing I had to talk about Mama's funeral with people I hardly knew. I walked over to the window while they talked.

"When do you go home?" asked the pastor.

"That's up to me, according to them."

The old man paused long enough for a nugget of hope to start growing inside me, at least for the kids. He sounded like he wanted to go home now, and he seemed to like Missy.

"The therapist said if I keep working like I did today, I could be home for good before Christmas. And I can go to the funeral, if someone will give me a ride."

"I'm sure Faith or Sam will do that for you," said the pastor.

I had to remind myself he was talking about Shenia's parents.

Then the funeral director showed up. We sat down at a table to work out the arrangements.

"Mama wanted to be cremated," I told them. At least I knew that. "She wanted her ashes scattered. That's what we did with Swede's."

"Your grandmother was the same way, but I kept some, in a pretty little box. It's in our bedroom. Do you think we could put some of your mother's in there, too, so they can be together?" the old man asked.

"Sure," I said. It came out a little tight, because my throat was choked up.

"You want to have a viewing first?" asked the funeral director.

"That's what we did with Swede."

"Fine with me," said the old man.

The rest went fast. We both agreed with everything they had figured out. The funeral director would put a simple notice in the paper Tuesday and Wednesday and there would be one viewing right before the funeral service, which we'd do at the funeral parlor instead of the church. We'd get her ashes a day or two later and we could take care of them whenever we were ready.

"The choir will be there," the pastor said.

"Lynnie sang in the church choir when she was young," the old man said. "Could you have them sing *Amazing Grace*? It was her favorite. She sounded like an angel singing it."

I'd never known Mama to sing, except once in a while with the car radio. Never loud enough to tell how good she was, though. It suddenly occurred to me that she'd had a whole life before I was born that I didn't know anything about.

The pastor and funeral director said goodnight and left the two of us alone together.

"Mr. Brown should be back soon," I told the old man.

"Actually, I asked him to wait until I call."

"Why?"

"We need to talk."

I didn't say anything. If he wanted to talk, he could talk. Instead, he motioned for me to follow and rolled back to his room, where he pulled a jacket off his bed.

"Help me get this thing on. I need to get outside."

I helped him get it tucked down behind him in his chair.

"You going to be warm enough in that sweatshirt?" he asked.

"Sure. You want me to push you?"

"If you would. Therapist wore me out today. I need to get my arms stronger to use that walker. It's like being a baby again, needing all fours to get around," he complained.

As I rolled him down the hall, I asked, "Will you always need the walker?"

"I'm not planning on it," he said. "Doctor said the bone healed, so it's up to me."

"You won't be needing help for long, then." I pushed the blue handicap button and the door opened for us.

"Just follow the walkway around the grounds. They bring me out here in the day sometimes, but I always liked evening the best, when there's still a little pink in the sky. We used to go down by the lake with your mother and watch the sun sink into the water."

I didn't know what to say. Mama had never talked about her childhood at all. What I wanted to ask was if he'd be taking the kids, but I was afraid asking might make him say no.

"I threw out your stocking last Christmas." His voice broke and he took a sharp breath. "Angelina was so mad at me. I told her she'd wasted our lives waiting for Lynnie to come home, that it was time to give up. And I threw out your stocking. She gave up. The cancer was diagnosed in January and she passed on in May."

"She didn't get cancer because of that."

"But it didn't help, and it was always there between us, all the way to the end. There was no way for me to make it up to her."

No wonder he was still grieving so hard. Without thinking, I blurted out my own confession. "I yelled at Mama the night before she died. I hate not being able to take it back."

He reached up to where my hand was and covered it with his.

"They're together now. I've got to believe they've forgiven us."

The anger boiled up and poured out of me before I even knew it was coming. "You mean like you forgave Mama for marrying my father?"

I yanked my hand out from under his and left him there.

The old man wheeled himself back to his room slowly. He found the slip of paper with the phone number on it and called Sam Brown's cell. "You'd better come get him. He doesn't want to talk with me anymore tonight."

"What happened?"

"Nothing. It's my fault."

"Let me talk to him," said Brown.

"He's out in the parking lot, waiting for you."

"He took off on you? I'll bring him in when I get there."

"No, he needs some time to himself," said Dolan.

"You're sure?"

"I started all wrong. I'll think through what I'm going to say better and try again tomorrow."

"Okay. I'll come get him."

"He's a good kid. You were right about that."

-70-

I was about to go in and apologize when Mr. Brown pulled up.

I expected him to chew me out for being rude to the old man, but he just pushed the door open without a word. Neither of us said anything the whole ride. I figured I'd blown it for sure and the kids were going to end up in foster care, but I didn't dare ask.

When we got back to the house, they were waiting dinner for us. Shenia had made a casserole after school and baked some of those rolls that come in a tube. It was apparently the normal routine for her when her parents were working.

I'd never thought of her that way, as part of a family depending on each other.

While we were cleaning up after dinner, all I could think of was how I'd probably blown it by getting mad at the old man. I was relieved that Shenia didn't try to get me to talk. She seemed to be off in her own place, too.

Once we were done cleaning the kitchen, Mrs. Brown had the little kids get ready and head to bed.

"You can read a little while," she said. "But you have another early day tomorrow, so only a few minutes."

"I'm beat, too," I said. "I'm gonna clean up and go to bed, too."

"Good idea," said Mrs. Brown.

Shenia didn't say anything. She must have been downstairs when I got done with my shower. It would have been nice to get a hug or something, but she probably would have wanted to talk, too.

So I didn't go downstairs. I got into my sweats and went to bed.

Jimmy was still awake and he kept chattering at me about the house and *our* room. I didn't tell him again that room was for *me.* I curled up with my back towards him and didn't say anything.

He finally shut up and fell asleep.

Then I let the tears roll for my grandmother, who'd loved me without ever knowing me.

Shenia realized her parents were locking up for the night. She shut down her computer and packed her bag for school.

"I caught up everything I missed last week."

"In one day?" her mother questioned.

"I started yesterday. Most of my classes post the work online."

"And I thought you were surfing the net."

Shenia turned away abruptly and headed up the stairs.

"Goodnight, Daddy," she said as she passed him.

"Goodnight."

He turned to his wife. "What was that about?"

"I said the wrong thing again. Plus she didn't want to go to school today. She wanted to help Michael watch the children."

"Should I be sleeping in the hallway between them?"

"I hope not."

"They weren't doing anything while they were on the road," he assured her.

"You're sure?"

"Not with the little ones right there, sleeping in the car."

"I don't know." She looked up the stairs. "You saw them last night, when they came in from that walk."

"Maybe I will sleep in the hallway."

"But actually, Michael pretty much ignored her tonight."

"He had an argument with his grandfather. I'm not sure what was said. Mr. Dolan wants to handle it himself tomorrow."

"That's probably why Shenia was so touchy with me; she's miffed at Michael for ignoring her."

"He's got a lot to deal with right now. You should talk to her about that, woman to woman."

Brown put his arm around her and they started up the stairs.

"Maybe later," she said. "I think I'd rather let her be annoyed with him while they're sleeping in the same house."

"You may be right."

Tuesday: Ups and Downs

-72-

When the cop drove off with the three kids, Carmella cautiously pulled out behind him. She'd never tailed anyone before, but she'd watched plenty of movies. She stayed back several car lengths, following each turn he made. Suddenly they were back at his house. He parked on the street across from it and got out of the car.

Her knuckles whitened as she increased her grip on the steering wheel. She had to drive past him or it would be suspicious. She looked in the rearview mirror and saw him looking at her drive away. He was probably getting her plate.

Now the cops would be after her.

She looked over at the empty car seat. Lester always could read her; he'd known she was going to take off as soon as he saw her yesterday. That's why he made her leave the baby with him today. If she just picked an address and gave it to him, he'd know she was lying. She had to give him good information, today, before the cops came back.

She called Lester. "Is the baby okay?"

"It's fine. They leave yet?"

"What was your girlfriend's name?"

"Lynn, Lynn Johnson. What do you need that for?"

"I've got to go. They're moving."

She drove to the Coffee Station and sat with the newspaper. Maybe Lester's old girlfriend hadn't been buried yet. Carmella had crashed more than one funeral for free food. This time she could try to get information. She turned to the obituaries. Three Johnsons, but only one woman, with exactly three children listed as survivors, and a father who lived in Sacramento. Lester had never mentioned the woman having a father in town, but it had to be her. If not, he wouldn't find out until Carmella and the baby were long gone. She could get out of town while he was watching the funeral tomorrow.

She texted him the time and place.

-73-

Michael Dolan was moving across the floor slowly with a walker when Sam Brown came into the therapy room.

"That's wonderful!" the therapist cheered.

"Help me sit down before I fall down," the old man grumbled. He exhaled heavily as she helped him settle in the wheelchair, then noticed Brown watching. "My good leg's coming back fast, but the bad hip's still awfully weak," he complained.

"I'm glad to see you making so much progress," said Brown. "How soon can you go home?"

"What do you think?" the old man asked his therapist. "Have I moved it up any?"

"Another few weeks with this kind of progress, and you'll be clear to go home."

"Is there any way he could go sooner?" asked Brown.

"Why, what's wrong?" demanded Dolan.

"We believe the man who murdered your daughter knows where the children are staying. His sister tried to tail me this morning. We need to move them to another location. If you're not going to take them, they need to go into foster homes right after the service tomorrow."

-74-

I was washing dishes while the kids watched television. It was dark in the house with the curtains closed on all the front windows, and Jimmy was getting antsy.

There was a soccer ball upstairs, but I didn't dare let him kick it around the backyard. I wasn't sure how fragile all those trees and plants were. Then the doorbell rang and Jimmy raced for it. I caught up and covered his hand as he started to undo the locks.

"First we look out and see who it is," I said.

Jimmy rolled his eyes but stepped back so I could look out the peephole in the door.

"There's no one out there." My stomach knotted up.

Jimmy ran to the living room window and peeked out. "It's a kid. He's starting to walk away."

I let him open the door.

"Hey!" he called.

The kid turned around and came back up the walk. He looked to be a little younger than Jimmy, but older than Missy.

"Who are you?" he demanded. "Did Mr. Dolan move?"

"We're his grandkids," Jimmy answered.

"Is your mom the one Mrs. Dolan was always looking for?"

"Yeah." I cut into the conversation. "Who are you?"

"I'm Jake, I live over there." He pointed to one of the other houses on the cul-de-sac. "Where's Mr. Dolan? We haven't seen him in weeks. He never let his lawn get that long before, and then someone cut it."

"That was me," I said. "He's been in the hospital—broke his hip."

"Oh man, my mom's going to be really mad we didn't know. She promised your grandmother she'd look out for him. We haven't been able to do much, though. He doesn't like being bothered."

"You knew our grandma?" Missy had come up beside me.

"Yeah. She was real nice and her cookies were awesome. I'm sorry about her dying. Mr. Dolan's okay, but he's not real friendly. It's cool your mom's finally hooked up with him, though."

"Actually, our mother passed away last week," I told him.

"Whoa. That's awful... Will you live here now?"

"Nothing's decided yet. We've just been cleaning it up some for him. He's still in a nursing home."

"It would be cool if you moved here." The kid seemed blind to my looking different from the kids. "You play soccer?" he asked Jimmy.

"Yeah, forward."

"Awesome," said Jake. "I usually have to practice by myself."

"Where?" asked Jimmy.

"Here in the street or in the field by the school. It's not far. We had early release today. Hey, you wanna go kick a ball around?"

"Sure!"

"No," I said. "Mr. Brown said we should stay together for now."

"Who's Mr. Brown?" asked Jake.

"It's a long story, but for a few days we have to stay together and mostly inside."

I didn't want to say more with Missy standing right there, and besides, I didn't know this kid.

"Can we all go for a walk, though? By the river? The access is over just one street. It's really cool, and I can show you some wild kittens, if you promise not to get too close. The mother will move them if you do."

"Kittens! I bet they're Grandpa's!" Missy clapped her hands. "Please, Michael?"

She sounded like her normal self. I didn't want to squash that.

Besides, it was a beautiful sunny day. There wouldn't be many more like this for months. It wasn't like Lester would stumble into this neighborhood, and we'd been cooped up all day.

"As long as we stay together. Let me get the key and lock up."

It felt good to walk down the street like normal people. Over one street there was room for about six cars to park, and a trail up to the riverbank that ran behind the old man's yard.

We walked down the river path and Jake pointed out which fence was our grandfather's. From this side, I noticed there was one board loose at the bottom. I could fix that, but I didn't want to use the old man's tools without asking. I could bring the Explorer toolbox tomorrow.

We still hadn't heard the mechanic's verdict. It would feel like another death if Swede's car couldn't be fixed. I shook off that feeling to yell at the boys, who were down by the edge of the water.

"Stay back! The current will take you right away if you fall in."

"I never fall in," said Jake. "There's a good place for swimming, but it's up the other way and it's way too cold this time of year."

Missy was holding my hand. "Where are the kittens?"

Jake led us to a grassy depression under a bush. There was some fur in it. "Darn, she must have moved them."

I hoped he was right. There had to be a lot of predators that would find them if a boy could.

Jake and Jimmy bounced on down the trail. They seemed like a good match. If the old man took in the kids, at least Jimmy would have someone to play with.

And just in case, I'd checked the Light Rail schedule I had in my pack. If I ended up living here, I could still get back and forth to visit Shenia. Of course, the way I'd talked to him, that probably wouldn't happen.

The boys came back to us.

"Jake says Grandpa has strawberries in the backyard," Jimmy said. "Did you see them? I didn't see them."

"There's a big patch along the back fence," said Jake.

"I saw them while I was mowing."

"Are there any ripe ones left?"

"I don't think so. They were buried in weeds and rotting fruit."

"Mr. Dolan always keeps them clean. He told me the plants are healthier that way."

"We can weed them," said Jimmy. "Grandpa will like that."

I figured *we* would end up *me* after a few minutes, but it was an easy way to get them back to the house.

Shenia cut across the student parking lot toward home. Her last class had tricked the sub into letting them out early.

A fat lot of good it was going to do Shenia, though. She was going to walk home, do her homework, and make dinner for everyone. Being grounded sucked.

The funeral was tomorrow morning. At least after that, Michael would be back at school and they could walk home together, unless her parents decided to keep them separate like they were now.

"Hey, girl, how you doing?" A hand reached out of a Mustang and brushed her arm. It was Will, one of Antoine's friends, from back when he was getting into trouble.

He had to be at least twenty, she thought. "What are you doing here?" Probably up to no good.

"Just waiting for some friends. You are looking good, girl. You're not a little kid anymore."

"No, I'm not." Shenia heard her mother's tone in her voice.

"Ouch. That mean you don't have the hots for me anymore?"

"That was kid stuff," said Shenia.

"How's Antoine doing?" Will asked.

"Good, he's doing good."

"Heard he got shipped over to the fighting?"

"Yeah."

"That's cool."

She didn't think Antoine would agree that it was cool, but she still said, "Yeah."

"Want a ride home? If you don't mind waiting for my friends."

"No thanks, I can walk."

"I won't bite. You're Antoine's kid sister. He'd kill me."

Shenia was about to say no again when it occurred to her that she might like a ride after all. She checked her back pocket and found Mr. Dolan's address, copied from her mother's planner.

"Would you mind running me across town?"

"No problem."

Her daddy was picking up Michael and the kids at four. That would still give her time to make dinner and with the funeral being tomorrow, she could put off most of her homework.

Why should she have to work all afternoon?

Besides, if Michael saw her ride up with Will and his friends in that Mustang, he might stop ignoring her.

Lester held the newspaper up in front of his face as her brats passed. They never even looked his way. He could have been driving his old car. But this piece of junk he'd picked up wasn't registered in his name or Carmella's, so the cops couldn't track him.

He glared at Michael's back. That kid kept growing.

He'd need to get the girl when she was off by herself. They couldn't stay together forever. She had to go to school sooner or later.

So Lynn did have a father in town. Carmella had even found the right address for him. Why the hell hadn't Lynn ever mentioned him? The old guy had to be loaded to live in this neighborhood.

Lucky for Lester there was that park along the river.

Once he figured out which house he wanted from the back, it would be easy to watch and wait for his opportunity to grab the little girl. All he'd have to do is chuck her in the river. Then it would look like an accident without him even having to try.

As long as the cops didn't get too close, he could take his time.

77

There had to be a hundred feet of strawberries. They ran the full length of the old man's back fence, except they were interrupted every few yards by a fruit tree. I'd had to throw lemons and apples off the lawn to mow. Now Jake showed us where the wheelbarrow was and the compost bin where he said we should put the rotten fruit. I'd wondered what that thing was. It was a long metal barrel with a handle at the end. Jake said you used that to turn the garbage so it would decompose completely.

There were oranges starting to ripen and the lemon tree that was still loaded in spite of all the ones on the ground. Those trees weren't labeled and they were bigger than the others, so I figured they'd been here when our grandparents bought the place. There was also a cherry tree with three different tags on it for different varieties, a Babcock peach, and the Cortland apple that had made an awful a mess.

"I remember your grandpa planting that apple tree," said Jake. "There was another before that one, but it died. I wish we'd known he was in the hospital. I'd have come over to get some apples and my mom would have made him a pie, and us, too. He said those apples make the best pies, and they do. Your grandma always made one for my family."

I wanted him to shut up. Those memories should have been mine. But Jimmy and Missy kept asking him more questions.

"Have you ever been upstairs?"

"Sure, when your grandma babysat for me when I was little."

"You're still little," I snapped.

Jake seemed oblivious to my mood. "I mean before I went to school. She'd put me down for a nap in their room, that little."

"What about the other rooms?" It was like I was poking myself in a sore spot with a stick. I didn't really want to hear that my room hadn't been so special after all, that this stranger had been allowed to play with the things meant for me, but I needed to hear it at the same time.

"Oh, the other doors were always closed. Are they open now?"

Jimmy told him all about the rooms that were waiting for us.

"You want to see?" he asked.

"No!" I yelled. "I told you, we weren't invited to go upstairs and we definitely shouldn't take other people up there, especially if they always kept those rooms closed. Are you going to help clean up these strawberries or not?"

Jimmy picked up an apple and slammed it into the wheelbarrow against the others.

"Um, I should get home," said Jake. "I've got some homework to do before dinner. I'll see you tomorrow?"

"We'll be at our mother's funeral tomorrow," said Jimmy. "I'm not sure if we're coming over here after that or not."

"But you'll be coming to live with your grandfather, right?"

There was a loud silence before I answered for Jimmy. "We're really not sure whether he can have us live here or not, with his broken hip and all. We may be going into foster care."

"Oh." Jake looked very uncomfortable. "That sucks."

No one argued with him.

"Well, if you come visit or anything, let me know." He headed for the gate.

I stood up and brushed the grass off my knees. My jeans were stained green. So were my fingers, from pulling weeds where we'd cleared away the fruit. All for an old man who would probably cut us out of his life just like he had Mama, an old man who'd been living in this big house with its beautiful yard while Mama was out there alone trying to take care of us. She hooked up with Lester because she was desperate. That had to be the reason.

"Stay in the backyard, kids," I called.

They ignored me and followed Jake through the gate to the front. I shouldn't have agreed to the walk along the river. They were going to be careless now. I went after them.

"Come on back here," I called.

The bass vibrations reached me before I realized a car had pulled up where I couldn't see it.

"Shenia's here!" cried Missy, and both kids took off.

I ran after them, sure they were wrong, sure that it was Lester somehow. But it wasn't.

Shenia was standing by a Mustang filled with guys, leaning on the edge of the open window.

"Thanks for the ride, Will."

"You got my number," the driver answered. "Call me."

She smiled and waved as the Mustang pulled away. Missy and Jimmy were hanging on her as if they hadn't seen her in years.

"Come on," I said. "You're not supposed to be out front."

And I turned and walked to the gate and stood there waiting for them while they pulled Shenia along, chattering to her about the cat and the river walk and the strawberries. They didn't notice I hadn't even said hello.

I couldn't tell if it bothered Shenia. I wasn't looking at her.

78

"Please, Michael? Can I please show Shenia the rose room?" Missy pleaded.

They'd already shown her the backyard and everything downstairs.

"He only asked us to take care of things down here. You heard Jake, those rooms were always closed. Private."

At least she'd called it the rose room instead of her room. I was afraid Missy was going to be crushed if the old man didn't at least take her and Jimmy. After the way I'd snapped at him last night, I knew he wouldn't want me around.

"We won't touch anything. I promise, please?"

Jimmy joined her. "Shenia's practically our family, and she's not going to tell, are you?"

"No, I won't say a word," she said.

"Fine, but just a quick look, then come right back down."

I didn't go with them.

We'd picked up the living room pretty good. I started loading the dishwasher and soaking pans. When I went through the living room to check for any more cups, I heard Jimmy showing her *our* room, too. I wanted to holler at him that it was *my* room, our grandmother hadn't even known he existed. She made that room for *me*.

Instead, I went back to the kitchen, got the dishwasher going, and started scrubbing pots. They came back down a few minutes later and Shenia got the kids settled in with a TV show before she came into the kitchen area.

"The kids told me about that pretty river walk." She sounded flirty, like she had when she was talking to that guy in the Mustang. "Why don't you show me while they're busy watching their show?"

I whispered. "We're here because Missy's in danger. I'm not leaving them alone."

"That man has no idea where you are, so why not?"

Her whisper was angry. I didn't care. I was angry, too.

"No," I said. "I'm cleaning up some more. If the old man comes by here after the service tomorrow and it looks good, maybe he'll take the kids. Otherwise we'll all be in foster care by the end of the week."

"Don't be silly. You're staying at my house until he gets better and can bring you here."

"He hasn't said he's taking any of us."

"He will."

"Maybe. But don't be getting the kids' hopes up. They've been hurt enough."

"Well, can we at least go sit in the garden and talk?"

"No, I really want to get the place cleaned up."

She glared at me, then went searching cupboards and slamming them shut while she fussed at me.

"Fine. You want to clean, we'll clean. Daddy won't be here for an hour or more."

She finally found the one with all the stuff for cleaning. I could have told her if she'd asked. She pulled out some cleaners and rags and kept looking until she found a vacuum.

"Kids," she called. "We're going to make this place shine for your granddaddy."

She had Missy polish chair legs and Jimmy the higher parts while she vacuumed. She came into the kitchen once, to put away the vacuum cleaner and get stuff to clean windows, but neither of us said a word.

I scrubbed those pots and pans and the nasty kitchen shelves and cleaned all the cupboard doors and wiped the inside of the refrigerator and cleaned the stove top, too.

It didn't look like he'd used the oven, so I left that alone and went after the floor. I was dumping the mop water when Mr. Brown arrived.

"How did you get here?" he asked Shenia.

"Will gave me a ride."

"Will!" He didn't sound any happier than I felt. "That boy is bad news. You don't know what he might have in that car or where he might take you."

"Don't worry, Daddy. I'm not hanging out with him or anything. He just happened to be at school when I was leaving and I wanted to come over here and help them get the place ready for their grandfather."

"She's a slave driver," Jimmy said.

Mr. Brown looked at me, then Shenia. He must have seen we weren't getting along, because he didn't ask any more questions.

"The place does look better," he said. "Wash up. I'm taking you to see your grandfather before we go home."

Home for him and Shenia. We didn't have a home.

79

The old man was in physical therapy when we got there.

"You can wait in the recreation room," the lady told us. "I'll go get him for you."

"Michael, you go with her," said Mr. Brown. "Tell him we can wait until he's done."

I was pretty sure he wanted to give me a chance to apologize for the way I acted the night before, so I followed her through the halls until she pointed out the therapy room. The old man was walking between low parallel bars, then with a walker.

"Excellent, Mr. Dolan," urged the therapist.

She reminded me of a cheerleader. A cheerleader with brown skin! He seemed friendly with her. Of course, she wasn't his family.

"You are doing so much better! You'll be leaving that wheelchair behind in no time."

Then he saw me. "Michael, come on over here and rescue me from this sadist."

I'd been hanging by the door, not sure I should interrupt.

The therapist smiled and waved for me to come over. "I'm done with him... Is this your grandson?"

"He's the older boy." He sounded almost proud. "He's been taking good care of his little brother and sister."

"Michael, watch how we transition your grandfather to his chair from the walker."

I wasn't sure why I needed to watch, but I did. She brought the chair close behind him, made sure the wheels were locked, then spotted him as he carefully shifted his weight from the walker to the chair, then lowered himself into the seat.

"You have to be careful the walker doesn't pop up and plop him down," she explained.

"I'm not going to use this thing much longer, anyway," he said.

"You'll keep it around for anytime you're exhausted."

"Won't happen. I'm not going to be a cripple."

He reminded me of Mama when she first got laid off.

"The kids are in the recreation room," I told him.

"Well, let's go then," he said.

He took off pushing himself. I had to catch up to apologize.

"I'm sorry for being rude and taking off on you last night, sir."

"Don't worry about it. I stuck my foot in my mouth. We can ask Brown to take the little ones home and finish our talk tonight."

I wasn't excited about that, but it would probably be my only chance to convince him he should take the kids. Missy greeted him like it was a done deal. It would break her heart if he let her go to foster care. I better do a good job talking.

"This is my daughter, Shenia, Mr. Dolan."

"Nice to meet you," said Shenia.

"You're the girlfriend?" he asked.

Jimmy answered before Shenia could say anything. "Yeah. She made us polish your furniture and everything today. And Jake came over. They didn't know you'd been hurt. They were wondering where you were when your grass got so long and everything."

The old man looked at my knees. "You did some yard work, too, from the looks of your jeans."

"We came straight over here, I didn't have a chance to change."

"Honest work's nothing to be ashamed of," he said. "I appreciate the effort."

"Jake told us to put all the rotten fruit in the compost bin, was that right?" asked Jimmy.

"It'll do."

"My wife said she'll pick you up for the service tomorrow," said Mr. Brown. "Her car will be easier for you to get in and out of than mine. She's also planning on making dinner for everyone."

"Mrs. Brown is an awesome cook," said Jimmy.

"Really?" the old man said. "I thought she said that she worked with lawyers."

"She's a good cook, too," said Mr. Brown.

"Well, tell her thank you."

"Speaking of dinner, we need to get home," said Mr. Brown. "Would you mind coming back for Michael later?"

"I'd be glad to."

Then they were gone and I was alone with the old man.

80

This was my only chance to talk him into taking the kids.

I figured I should start by letting him finish what he was saying the night before. Even if he made me mad again, I was going to stay calm and polite. I had to, for the kids. I followed him to an empty office. He pointed to a chair.

"Sit down, Michael," the old man said. "We have some things we need to talk out."

I sat and kept my mouth shut. He wheeled around to face me, eye to eye. It seemed like he took forever to start talking.

"You're right about me, and wrong." He glanced away, took a breath, then turned back, sitting straight. "It's true, I did not like your father. And I didn't want my grandchildren to have to deal with the prejudice I'm sure you've encountered being mixed race."

He paused to see if I would say anything, but I was determined to hear him out politely. Besides, I *had* been called names by black and white. Mostly ignorant people, though.

"She wouldn't listen. She got herself pregnant and ran off with your father. Whenever she called and talked to her mother, I wouldn't get on the phone. Then one day your grandmother was out. I was the only one there to answer it. I thought Angelina had forgotten something. But it was your mother, saying your father had died in a barroom brawl. She wanted to come home and I should have said yes."

He was tearing up. I was feeling a little shaky myself.

"I should have said yes, but it was the first time I'd talked to her since she'd left and all the hurt and anger spilled out of me until she hung up. My first thought was to call her back, but I couldn't find her number, didn't know where your grandmother had it. Then when Angelina came home, I was ashamed to tell her how I'd acted."

"You didn't tell her Mama had called or anything?" I asked.

"No," he said miserably. "We were packed to leave on the first vacation we'd ever had. She tried calling your mother before we left, but she wasn't there, so Angelina left a cheerful message about how we'd be out of town for a month."

He stopped talking to blow his nose.

Mama had thought her mother knew about my daddy dying and didn't care. But she hadn't known.

"When we got back," he continued, "your answering machine wasn't working and Angelina never managed to call while your mother was there. Then the number was disconnected. When your mother didn't call with a new one, I finally told Angelina what had happened. She went down there to try and find you, but no one had a forwarding address."

"We moved out here with Swede. A friend of his had lined up a good job for him."

"All we knew was she'd taken off with some man. I called her a tramp." He choked out the words.

I had to defend her, but I tried to be fair, too. "Maybe it was a little quick, but Swede was a good man, and she knew he'd take care of us. He always treated me like his own."

"Your grandmother reamed me out when I talked that way, said I had no idea what it was like for a woman alone with a child."

"She didn't sleep around." He needed to know that. "Lester's the only one she hooked up with after Swede died. I don't know why him, though."

"You said she'd lost her job."

"Yeah, she'd been looking for another for the better part of a year when they hooked up. Maybe he did help pay the bills, but I didn't like him from the start, so I wasn't around much to see what he was doing."

"You did your best to protect her," he said.

"I wish we hadn't argued that way her last night."

"And I wish I hadn't been such a fool on the phone with her."

"Swede was a good father, and the kids wouldn't exist if we'd come to live with you."

"Think you can forgive me?" the old man asked.

I nodded. I knew he was right the night before—Mama would have forgiven both of us.

"Will you move in with me, then? You and the kids?"

"You want all of us?" I wasn't sure I'd heard right.

"You have your mother's eyes, Michael. Makes it hard for me to look at you sometimes. But I'm proud to say you're my grandson, the way you've watched out for those children."

"We're really going to live with you?"

"Yes."

"All of us?"

"All of you."

He meant it. If I tried to thank him, I was going to start bawling. I could feel it pushing up inside me. Instead, I asked, "When?"

"I'm checking out tomorrow."

"The doctor said you're ready?"

"No. He insists I still need assistance available around the clock, so I'm hiring a health aide for the hours you're all in school. He'll get me over here for my therapy sessions, and I'm getting a whole pile of other exercises I have to do, too."

"Wouldn't it be better to stay until the doctor says you're ready?"

"I can't sleep with that new roommate. And I don't know if Brown had a chance to talk to you alone, but we need to get you out of their house altogether. That man's sister was there this morning and tried to follow you to our house."

Our house.

Mr. Brown returned a missed call while he waited for Michael.

"Schuster."

"This is Sam. You called?"

"Yeah. We talked ourselves into a warrant for the sister, since she seemed to be stalking our key witness."

"And?"

"She's packed up and gone. Not everything, but what I'd expect her to fit into that car. We've put out an alert for the plates, but I doubt we'll see her again."

"Any sign of him?"

"We're pretty sure he was staying there, but he probably won't come back either. Not if he realizes we got a search warrant."

"Did you find anything to add to your case?"

"No. Sorry."

"Think you'll be able to put him away when you find him?"

"It would be better if we could get the sister back here and she would admit he coerced her into helping after the fact."

-82-

It was our last night with the Browns.

My mind was racing around way too fast to sleep, thinking about Mama, and that room that had been there waiting for me all this time, and worrying about when they were going to catch Lester. I didn't even want to get my hands on him myself anymore. I just wanted to know that Missy was safe. So I was wide awake when the door eased open.

"Michael?" Shenia whispered.

I almost died then and there. She put a finger to her lips and gently pulled my hand to get me out of bed and into the hallway.

"Step next to the wall," she breathed into my ear at the top of the stairs.

She was still holding my hand. What saved me was she had a big terrycloth bathrobe over top of her pajamas. I was in a pair of sweatpants and no shirt. She motioned for me to wait at the bottom of the stairs, then went and got a little blanket off the couch and wrapped it around my shoulders.

"Come on back to the kitchen," she whispered. "My parents won't hear us there."

We sat on the floor against the wall, side by side, holding hands.

"Are we still going to be boyfriend and girlfriend?" she asked.

"What about Will?"

"He's an old friend of my brother's. I was just flirting to try and get you to pay attention. You'd been ignoring me."

"Not on purpose. There's been a lot distracting me, you know."

"I know."

"I didn't even know for sure you wanted to be my girlfriend."

"I was so scared you'd end up living across the country, but I still had to help you. Do you think I'd have gotten myself into that much trouble if I didn't like you?"

"Yeah, I guess not... Thanks. I don't know where we'd be if you hadn't jumped in and helped like that. I felt like a zombie at first."

"I know. It had to have been awful."

"You really want to be my girlfriend?"

"Yeah."

"I'm going to be in a different high school now, but the Light Rail comes over here."

"And you'll get your license soon."

"The Explorer's dead. Your dad told me when he brought me back here tonight."

"Your grandfather will probably let you drive that old truck he's got, don't you think?"

"Maybe."

I was going to just sit there like that, side by side, holding hands. Then she leaned against me and rested her head on my shoulder, and that felt good, too. Somehow my free hand came over and her face came up and my head turned some and then there we were, lying on the floor by each other kissing hot and heavy, pressing up against each other and I wasn't even embarrassed for her to know what she was doing to me.

I slipped my hand under her robe and was sliding it down to press her against me more, and her pajamas were so thin it was like there was nothing there and then CRASH went something behind the house and we heard footsteps upstairs and we jumped up and she pulled her robe shut and I made sure I was covered with the blanket and over by the table while she reached up in the cupboard for a couple mugs and set them on the counter as her father came into the room in nothing but his boxers carrying his service revolver. And he saw us there in the kitchen with no light except the glow from the LCD on the microwave and the starlight coming in the window.

"Did you knock something over?" he hissed at us.

"No," Shenia whispered. "It was behind the house."

He went out the door like they do on cop shows, standing sideways, holding his gun ready. It was only a moment or two before he came back into the kitchen.

"The garbage can's tipped over. Probably a raccoon." He turned on the overhead light. "So, what do you two think you're doing?"

I let Shenia do the talking. "I couldn't sleep so I came down to make some cocoa and Michael was here. He'd come downstairs to get some water without waking people up. You know how noisy that bathroom sink is, Daddy."

He didn't look he believed her.

"We were just talking, Daddy. Really."

I bobbed my head up and down, not trusting myself to speak.

"Sam?" her mother called quietly from upstairs. "Are you okay?"

He looked hard at each of us in turn, then put it back on Shenia.

"Your mother will be calling 911 if I don't get back upstairs right now. The two of you will have to do without your cocoa."

He pointed the way and we went back to our own beds.

I didn't sleep at all the rest of the night. I was thirsty, but I couldn't go to the bathroom.

I would have had to step over Mr. Brown.

Wednesday: Saying Goodbye

-83-

We were burying Mama on Veteran's Day, so Shenia didn't even have to argue with her parents to be with us all day.

Right after breakfast was cleaned up we all went over to the apartment carrying empty boxes. The yellow tape was gone. We could get the rest of our things.

Mr. Brown made sure Mrs. Brown and I had our cell phones on us. I was still using the prepaid one that we'd bought on the road. We hadn't gotten back the ones we threw into the pickup, so Shenia didn't have one. She wasn't very happy about that.

The priority was cleaning out the apartment so we wouldn't have to go back where Lester might see us. We didn't want him to follow us and find out where we were living now. That's why we were taking care of it before the funeral.

"Sorry we have to rush this," said Mr. Brown.

We weren't mentioning Lester in front of Missy. She'd already been scared enough.

"It's better to get it over with anyway," I said.

"Is the furniture yours?" asked Mrs. Brown.

"Yes, ma'am. It's all ours. From our house."

"Is there anything you want to keep? I didn't go upstairs at your grandfather's. Are the bedrooms furnished or will you need your own beds? We can get a truck."

"He's got everything we'll need," I said. "I guess we'll sell the rest, or donate it."

"You can decide that with your grandfather and then we'll take care of the arrangements, if you leave the key with me," offered Mrs. Brown.

"I want to keep Mama's treasure chest," said Missy.

"Sure," I said. "Mama would want you to have that. Let's go empty it out so it's easier to move. Then you can box up whatever you want from inside."

"What about dishes or other kitchen things?" asked Mr. Brown.

"The mugs," I said. "We have a lot of special mugs."

"And there's the Snoopy spoon we had when we were babies," said Jimmy. "I'll take care of the kitchen while you guys go upstairs. I mainly want the pictures we already took to Shenia's house. I got all my stuff before."

"Okay, but check when you're done in the kitchen," I told him.

Mr. Brown went to help Jimmy. Shenia and her mother went with Missy and me to Mama's bedroom. Someone had cleaned up. I'd been afraid there'd be chalk lines and such, but the bed was stripped down and the mattress was gone.

I nodded toward the bed as I asked Mrs. Brown, "Did you folks take care of that?"

"Sam knew some people who clean up in situations like this."

"Thank you."

Missy was doing okay, maybe better than me.

"So, is this the treasure chest?" Mrs. Brown asked her.

"Yes. It has Mama's special things in it."

It was a four foot cedar chest that would fit into the rose room for Missy, maybe under another window, like in that closet. Together we went through Mama's treasures. On top of a towel were samples of our art work from school, little clay handprints, Mother's Day cards, stuff like that. Mrs. Brown said we should keep everything and she packed all of it in one of the boxes. Under the towel was an ivory satin dress with lace on it wrapped in tissue paper.

"That's beautiful," said Shenia.

"She wore it when she married my daddy," I said. It had always made me feel good that she kept it. That seemed to mean she'd loved him even if he ended up dying in a bar.

"No, Michael," said Missy. "Mama wore it when she married *my* daddy. She *told* me."

That was a lie. Mama and Swede were never legally married. I remembered them talking about it not being necessary. But maybe Mama had changed her mind after he was gone or maybe she didn't want Missy to know or maybe Missy needed to believe in a wedding.

So I said, "She probably wore the same dress for both, Missy. You know Mama was never wasteful."

"Can you do that?" she asked.

"Of course," said Mrs. Brown, with a look that made me think she knew exactly what I was doing, that our Mama had only ever had one wedding.

"Can I keep the dress?" asked Missy.

"Of course."

Mrs. Brown and Shenia moved it carefully to a box all by itself.

Underneath were photo albums of us growing up and her high school yearbooks.

"Grandpa will probably want to see these," I said, putting them all in the box with our art.

Most of the other things meant nothing to us. There were tickets and playbills, and an old diary from when she was a teenager.

"Box those up to keep, too," said Mrs. Brown. "Your grandfather may be able to tell you about some of it, and you might want to read the diary someday."

I wasn't sure that would be right, but I did as Mrs. Brown said.

All that was left was a little beaded purse. Missy picked it up. "Mama wouldn't let me play with this or her dress, but she said I could use the purse when I get big and go to prom."

She gasped and tears started pouring down her face as she pulled open the zipper. "I forgot," she sniffled. "I forgot what Mama told me."

"What, honey?" asked Shenia.

"She wrote a letter for Michael. It was a secret, but she said if Lester came back and she wasn't here, I should show you. I'm sorry. I forgot."

She pulled an invitation-sized envelope out of the purse and handed it to me.

"That's okay," I told her.

It was sealed, with no writing on either side.

"You think it's okay to open it?" I asked.

"We'd better ask Mr. Brown," said his wife.

We went down to the kitchen and I gave him the envelope. He held it by a corner as he called Martinez.

"It was hidden away," he said into the phone. "Not likely there'd be any fingerprints on it, if that would mean anything anyway... Okay."

Mr. Brown closed the phone and opened the envelope with a knife, still holding it by that corner.

It was personal to me. I didn't want someone else to read it.

"Get me some plastic wrap, Jimmy," he said. "And give Michael a couple pieces, too."

He used it to pull out an invitation to my parents' wedding. The letter was inside it, sticking out a little.

"Use the wrap to hold the letter, Michael. If there's anything they can use in court, we don't want extra fingerprints on it."

He held the invitation while I pulled out the letter. Everyone was staring at me, but I really wanted to read it alone.

Then Mrs. Brown said, "Go on upstairs, Michael. Tell us later what we need to know."

I took off before anyone else could put in their two cents.

Mrs. Brown may be a little scary sometimes, but she's okay. I went up to our old bedroom. Cross-legged on my bed, I carefully unfolded Mama's message with the plastic wrap, so I wouldn't leave any fingerprints.

> *Michael,*
>
> *Please forgive me for Lester. I was so stupid. At first he seemed to take care of us, but then I let him stay because I was afraid. I sent him away because I was even more afraid of what you might do, and how we would live with that. But he came back and I was too afraid not to let him.*
>
> *Missy walked in on us yesterday and I said I'd call the police. He said we were all dead if I did, then he killed Betsy, right in front of us. I was too afraid to call the police, afraid they wouldn't do anything about a dead cat. If you're reading this, he's probably killed me, and I hope to God I'm the only one. Please forgive me.*
>
> *I love all of you. Mama*

I went back downstairs and showed Mr. Brown. Martinez came to collect the note.

When we were done, everything we were taking fit into the back of Mr. Brown's Expedition, once we figured out to put things inside the chest for the trip. Martinez followed me and Mr. Brown to Grandpa's house, to make sure no one else was tailing us. We unloaded it all into the garage, then headed back to clean up for the funeral.

Mr. Brown went straight upstairs to shower. I wanted a glass of milk first. Mrs. Brown was in the kitchen frosting a cake.

"I've got everything for dinner ready to take with us, so you can eat in your own home tonight," she said as she covered the cake and put it into a box with a casserole dish and salad stuff. "Do you like macaroni and cheese?"

There was way too much churning around inside of me to try and answer.

"Are you okay, Michael?"

"I wish Mama never met Lester."

"She wished the same thing, child."

-84-

Grandpa was waiting in the lobby, dressed in church clothes, with his suitcase and folded-up walker next to his chair. His therapist was there handing him a fat folder.

"She's making me work between my formal therapy sessions," he complained.

I knew he wasn't really upset and so did she.

"Don't let him slide," she said. "I've included pictures of each movement and exercise your grandfather needs to do, and how often, how many sets and how many reps. Like weight lifting?"

I nodded. "I've done weights at school."

"It's the same principal. Both are building muscle to protect the joints. These are focused on your grandfather's hips, but it wouldn't hurt to do a full weight lifting program once he's a hundred percent again."

"Is there anything he shouldn't do?"

"Not really," she said. "It's not like he had a replacement or surgery, even. The bones were not displaced and they healed nicely on their own. He should regain full use. I've included yoga exercises also, to increase range of motion."

She flipped to the back of the folder. "These positions should only be approximated. Never force anyone into a yoga position. The idea is to gently go to one's limits on a regular basis, and gradually increase that range. It should never cause pain, only an ache like you feel after a good workout."

"I've done a few of those before," I told her.

"Good."

"What about stairs?" he asked. "I forgot to tell you my bedroom's on the second floor."

"Wait until we add a step to your therapy, then do one at a time. You don't want to push that too soon and have an injury set you back."

"Yes ma'am. Can I leave now?" he grumbled.

"Yes. Leave. See you next week."

I grabbed his suitcase and the walker. She pushed the button for the automatic door and Grandpa rolled himself to the Subaru while I put his things in the back.

Mrs. Brown was waiting with the heater running. It wasn't quite raining, but it was a gloomy day with a lot of moisture in the air. I hoped it wouldn't make him sick.

I hurried to open the door for him. "Do you need help getting into the car?"

"No," he said as he locked the brakes. "But I'll need you to fold the chair and put it behind the seat."

I still spotted his elbow as he shifted to stand, holding onto the chair and the car. Then he twisted his butt around and let it down into the seat. He bumped his head on the door frame.

"Oh dear!" Mrs. Brown exclaimed.

"No harm. It's an Irish skull. Thick. Probably why I was so rude to you when we first met."

He lifted one leg at a time into the car. Good thing we'd put the seat all the way back for him. While I figured out how to collapse his wheelchair, he apologized to Mrs. Brown.

"I am sorry about my behavior the other night."

"Apology accepted," she said. "Michael, do you need him to move up the seat to get that into the car?"

"I think so. You can move it back again when it's time to get out."

When I'd wrestled the chair into the car, I sat in the back behind Mrs. Brown. The two of them spoke to each other politely.

"The children and Shenia are riding with my husband."

"Thank you for helping out, Mrs. Brown, with the children and the service. When Angelina died, the ladies from her church took care of everything. I was in no shape to do anything but sit there while people offered condolences. They brought food to the house and we received everyone there. Do you think it's proper to be doing that at the funeral parlor?"

"It's perfectly suitable, Mr. Dolan," she reassured him.

The funeral parlor had a small parking lot next to the building. They wouldn't need remote parking like I'd seen in Reno, not for Mama.

"Is Missy going to be okay with the viewing?" Grandpa asked as I helped him into his wheelchair.

"She's been through it with her daddy already," I told him.

"Think she remembers?" he asked. "She's pretty young."

"I think so. She said she's got Mama's Christmas present to put in with her."

When we got inside, the pastor was already there, talking to Jimmy and Missy in a little side room with the door open.

"Michael, Mr. Dolan," he said. "Would you join us and share your memories?"

That's how we got to know what our mother had been like growing up. The pastor must have leaned towards viewing a life chronologically, because he asked Grandpa to start.

"I have so many memories of your mother as a little girl. She looked like you, Missy, but not quite as sweet as you. She was a real tomboy. Got into scrapes all the time."

"Like me," Jimmy interrupted.

"Did she tell you about that?" Grandpa asked.

"She told us the scar on her foot was from getting stitches."

Grandpa laughed. "We could never keep shoes on her when she was little. She was about five when she cut her foot wide open on something, we never did know what. She came back to the house, trailed blood all the way up the stairs to the bathroom, and washed it off herself. It didn't stop bleeding enough to put a Band-Aid on it, so she wrapped a hand towel around it and thought that was fine. Her mother was in the garden, weeding, and thought Lynnie was playing in her sandbox. I was out on the tractor somewhere. When we came in to lunch, there's this trail of blood already drying on the floor. Scared us both half to death. She was in her room, playing. The bleeding had eased up enough so she was okay, but the cut was too deep to heal without the stitches."

"Stitches can hurt worse than the cut," said Jimmy.

"I think that was the case," Grandpa said.

"What else did she do?" asked Jimmy.

"Well, when she was about your age, her cat got stuck up in a tree. Now a cat will eventually figure out how to come down, when it gets hungry enough, but Lynnie didn't want to wait. She was too worried about the stupid cat. So she climbed up after it and got onto a limb that could barely hold her and it ended up we had to get the extension ladder out and I had to climb up to rescue them both!"

"What else?" asked Missy.

"Well, she was a real go-getter in high school, voted most likely to succeed, always ready to help anyone who needed it."

"Did she sing in chorus like I do?" asked Missy.

"Yes she did," he said. "She was in chorus all the way through and sang with the church choir, too. In fact, Michael, she sang with a rock and roll band in college. That's how she met your father. He joined them as a drummer."

"I knew he played drums in a band. I didn't know Mama ever sang with them. How far did she get in college?" I asked.

"She dropped out the middle of her second year to get married."

"What was she going to be?" asked Missy.

"Well, she was majoring in Political Science. She talked about going into international relations, working overseas, or going on to law school. She could have."

"But instead she had me." It was my fault she never did any of those things.

"She always wanted to be a mother, Michael. The rest of it was talk. Every boy she ever met, she'd ask her mother if she thought he'd make a good husband and father. She was so happy you were on the way."

"Well, she was blessed with three children," said the pastor.

"She picked a really good husband and father. I don't remember much about mine, but Swede, the kids' dad, was awesome."

"Yeah," said Jimmy. "We all used to go on the river and Mama would pack the best lunches and double wrap them in plastic bags and put them in a cooler, and if they got wet, she'd be all upset, but they'd still taste good and we'd make her laugh about it."

"And she made us the best Halloween costumes," said Missy. "We never had stupid store-bought ones."

"She always had a garden, until we moved to the apartment," said Jimmy. "We'd have the best tomatoes."

"She saved our artwork in her treasure box," said Missy.

I thought about her note, explaining Lester.

"She loved us more than anything," I said.

The pastor did a nice job talking about Mama and then the choir sang beautifully. We all commented on that and thanked them after the service when we were doing the receiving, which was really just people standing around talking about Mama, or going up to look closer at her, or having some of the punch and stuff in a side room the funeral man had opened.

I walked up with Missy, holding her hand. She put a painting she'd made for Mama in with her, next to the clay bowl Jimmy had given her, both of them right where Mama could reach them.

Some of our old neighbors showed up, too. They were all glad to meet Grandpa and know we had someone to take care of us.

"We've been so worried about you kids, ever since we saw the funeral notice," said Swede's friend who'd gotten him the job that brought us to California in the first place. "We were trying to figure out how we could squeeze you all into our little house."

He turned to Grandpa and explained, "Between us we have seven children, and we're crammed into a three bedroom house. It's a good thing someone invented bunk beds."

"Grandpa has a three bedroom house with a really big yard," offered Missy. "We'll have lots of room."

"Well, maybe I should send a couple of mine over to keep you company," he said.

"Could Jenny visit?" Missy asked Grandpa. "We used to play all the time."

"When I'm back on my feet," he said.

Missy gave him a hug.

It was really happening. We were really going to live with him.

-86-

Lester tried on another pair of sunglasses as he watched them leave the funeral parlor. He'd parked just off the alley that ran behind the stores. If he had to, he could walk out through the back of the pharmacy. But he wouldn't need to do that. The cops were looking for someone sitting in a car out on the street. He wasn't that dumb.

At first he'd been furious when he came back from the river and found Carmella had packed up and left. He was in the basement storage room, looking to see if she'd taken everything, when the cops came back with their warrant. It was pure luck that she'd left the baby monitor and that it was still on and charged from when he'd hidden down there with Carmella's baby.

He heard everything they said in the apartment. The girl was the center of their case. As long as he got rid of the kid, it wouldn't matter if they found Carmella. She'd be too scared to talk.

He didn't really have to be here. But it seemed fitting to observe the funeral, from a safe distance. He knew where to find the girl. They'd end up at the old man's place soon. Who else would take in three kids? He was surprised the cop had kept them a week.

87

We all headed to Grandpa's house after the funeral. I rode with Mrs. Brown so I could help with the wheelchair again. Second time setting it up I was feeling confident already. I got it into position and locked the wheels. He ducked his head and used my arm to lift himself out of the car, then twisted and sat in the chair.

"Did that like we're pros!" he crowed as he turned to face his house. "It's good to be home. I was stuck in that place and the hospital for too long."

"Do you need help with the food?" I asked Mrs. Brown.

"No, I have a call to answer. You go on with your grandfather. I'll wait for Sam to get here with the others."

Grandpa was already pushing himself up the front walk. "You did a nice job with the outside, Michael. I'll need some help getting over the threshold, I think."

There was a small rise to go over where the door closed, so he did need a little push to go up, over, and into the house. At least there were no steps. He stopped just inside.

"It's beautiful." His voice cracked a little. "You kids did a great job cleaning the place up. I'm sorry it was such a pigsty."

"It didn't take that long."

"Thank you anyway. You know, part of my not wanting to come home was thinking about what a dump it had become and realizing I wouldn't be able to maneuver in a wheelchair or walker."

"That's what we figured."

"After Angelina passed, I couldn't stand being in the house. Spent all my time in the yard and slept in the recliner. I haven't been upstairs since the funeral. Kept washing the same clothes to avoid going up there and seeing all her things. Don't do that with your mother's belongings."

"We already brought over everything we want to keep. It's in the garage. There were some things we figured you'd want to see, too," I said. "But the Browns are boxing up the stuff we left, since we can't go back to the apartment. Then we'll donate it somewhere."

"Maybe you can box up your grandmother's things for me later this week. They could get rid of it all at once."

"We can do that, and we'll bring stuff down here for you to sort. Should we bring a bed downstairs for you?" I asked.

"Nah, I like sleeping in my recliner. I'd say you could have the big bedroom, Michael, but I'm thinking once my hip's doing better, I'll want to have it for myself. I'm not used to sharing the house anymore; I might need a place to hole up if I want to be alone."

"That's okay. I'm used to sharing a room with Jimmy."

I took him out back to see his yard.

He started rolling himself along the path. "I never liked this cement walk, but it's sure handy now."

I thought it was nice how it curved around and connected things. There was even a branch off to the living room's sliding glass door.

When we got over by the deck he had me pull some leaves out of the fountain and drop them on the ground beside a rose bush. "I won't be in this chair long enough to bother putting in a ramp for that little rise to the deck, and I can roll out there from the kitchen. That deck was your grandmother's favorite spot. It's closer to the street, but you don't hear the highway so much."

"It's quiet here," I told him.

He laughed. "You've grown up with it. These freeways have cars humming down them night and day. Where we used to live, there was only one major road and it wasn't half this busy. I wanted a place farther out when we got here, but they were too expensive, and Angelina wanted to be in the city."

"She did?"

"She thought she might run into your mother in a store or on the street, or at the movies. She was always looking." He turned around and rolled back to the middle. "See how the yard goes up in the back? That's the only reason I bought next to the river. It would have to get over that to ever flood the house. The best thing about the place is the peepers drown out the traffic noise most nights."

When we went back inside, Mrs. Brown and Shenia were busy in the kitchen and the kids and Mr. Brown were carting our stuff from the garage up to our rooms and putting things away. Jimmy and I worked out who had what parts of the closet and stuff. I was going to share my room with Jimmy and I might as well get used to it.

It was still nice to know it had been sitting there waiting for *me*.

Jake came over when he saw us, and it was decided Jimmy could go to Jake's house, but nowhere else. We didn't explain the whole thing to Jake, but Mr. Brown pulled Jimmy aside to make sure he understood how important it was to be careful.

"Call when you're coming back," Mr. Brown told him. "Even though it's that close."

"Take the cell phone with you," I added.

"Okay." He put Grandpa's number in it before he left.

Mrs. Brown had dinner heating up in the oven, Shenia was busy helping her make a shopping list with input from Grandpa, and Mr. Brown went to look at the gardens.

I went back up to my room, our room, to have some time to myself without any decisions to make. On the way, I checked on Missy. She'd put all of her things away. Mama's dolls and stuffed animals from that box in the closet were lined up on the pillows of Missy's new bed.

"You going to have any room to sleep in there?" I teased.

"I left a spot in the middle. I'll slip in very carefully from the top."

She'd sleep right in the middle of memories from Mama.

I went and stretched out on my bed.

I could hear Missy having Mama's dolls talk to each other and murmurs from the kitchen. Dinner was making the house smell good, even though it was macaroni and cheese.

Mama would be glad we were safe and glad we'd found her father, even though her mother was gone. They were probably together now. She'd be glad we'd survived that crazy trip, too. And I was sure she'd like Shenia and be impressed how good she was with Missy, and how she could cook, and how much she did around the house and pitched in whenever anyone needed help without even being asked.

It was sad to be without Mama, but we were going to be okay.

For the first time since it all began, I felt like I could relax.

Mike Dolan pointed to a shelf next to the refrigerator. "Angelina's cookbooks are up there. The spiral notebook is her own recipes."

Mrs. Brown pulled out the spiral notebook and skimmed through several pages. "You and Michael will be able to follow these. She wrote detailed directions. And that white cookbook's a good one."

"It even tells you how to boil an egg," said Shenia.

He laughed. "I've boiled eggs."

"There's more than one way," Shenia replied defensively. "If you don't do it right, you get that nasty green layer on the yolk."

"Really, that's how you cook it, not the egg itself?" asked Dolan.

Shenia looked at her mother. "I think we should put frozen dinners on the list."

"We're not going to be that helpless," said Dolan. "I suppose some would be okay, but growing children need proper meals."

"So do you," said Shenia. "We had a big trash bag full of fast food containers when we cleaned up for you."

"You need to eat properly, too, Mr. Dolan," her mother agreed.

"Mike, please."

"Then call me Faith." She handed him the notebook. "Why don't you pick out some of your favorites, and we'll get the ingredients for them."

"We won't be canning, at least not this year." He flipped past several pages. "Here's her recipe for beef stew. Angelina made an awfully good stew. And her spaghetti sauce and lasagna recipes are in here, too."

"You'll be able to make those," said Mrs. Brown.

"Angelina was second generation Italian," he said. "Her mother scared the bejazus out of me when I first met her. Good cook, though. Most of those recipes came from her."

He read ingredients off and Shenia added items to their list.

"We'll pick those things up after dinner," said Mrs. Brown.

Dolan quickly sketched out a map. "Here's the grocery store. It's not far at all. Neither is the elementary school."

"Where's the high school?" asked Shenia.

"That's several blocks away," he said. "But wouldn't it be better for Michael to finish the semester where he is?"

"Really?" That was the best news Shenia had heard all day.

"Probably," said Mrs. Brown. "How would he get there?"

"Michael said the Light Rail runs out this way," said Shenia.

"He could make sure no one was following him, couldn't he?" asked Dolan.

"Sure," said Shenia.

"Who would get the children to and from school safely?" asked her mother.

"Well, they made me hire a health aide so I'm not going to be alone all day. Until they catch that guy, I'll have the aide run the kids to school and pick them up. Jake's mother might help, too." Dolan rolled himself over to the phone and looked on a sheet of numbers posted under it. "I'll call her. She should know the situation anyway, what with Jimmy going over there."

"Have her send Jimmy home now, too," said Mrs. Brown. "Shenia, set the table, then round up everyone for dinner."

-89-

Lester walked along the river.

He'd driven past the cul-de-sac earlier and seen both the Subaru and the Expedition in front of the old guy's house. He'd parked a couple blocks away in a little shopping plaza, figuring they'd pass that way to head back to their house.

After a couple hours, he began to wonder if he'd missed them somehow. He finally pulled out and drove by again.

Still there. It was full-on dark and there was a light on upstairs. The old guy was in a wheelchair when they came out of the funeral home. They wouldn't stay this long unless he was staying here now, and he wouldn't be upstairs. The kids had to be moving in with him. Lester parked at the river access and watched the street until he saw both of the Browns' cars pass by, with only the drivers and one passenger.

Now he walked down the river to the old guy's fence. He pushed on the broken board a bit and was able to see right into the living room through the sliding door across the back of the house. The old guy was staying up watching television, already set in his recliner for the night. He'd be easy enough, but that kid would be a problem.

The cops were close, and Lester wasn't sure where Carmella was or whether she'd talk if they got to her.

He'd try to catch the little girl alone or only the crippled old guy with her. He'd give that a couple days. If it didn't work, he'd have to burn the whole place down with all of them in it.

I laid in my bed breathing in the freshness of the sheets. Mrs. Brown had laundered them after dinner, while Shenia and I went for groceries with Mr. Brown and the kids played cards with Grandpa.

When she told us she was going to do that, part of me wanted to stop her so I could sleep one night on sheets that my grandmother had washed for me. But after sitting so long they *were* kind of musty, and Mrs. Brown used the end of Grandma's detergent. So this was probably more like my first night here would have been if she were still alive. My grandmother wouldn't have left the sheets musty. Strange, how I was feeling her absence more than Mama's. Maybe because we were able to say goodbye to Mama properly today, and I never even got to say hello to my grandmother.

Jimmy was sound asleep in the other bed. I'd taken first pick and he hadn't argued about it. Missy fell asleep on the couch and I carried her upstairs, with Shenia coming along to help get her into the middle of that big bed and line up all the dollies the way she'd had them. We snuck in a few kisses, but then Shenia's mother called for her to come down so they could leave.

I really needed to get to sleep. Taking the Light Rail to my old school meant getting up before dawn. It was only for a few weeks, though. A week and a half to the Thanksgiving break, then there were only three weeks left in the semester. After Christmas I'd be moving to my new high school, a better school. I wouldn't get to see as much of Shenia then, but for now we'd see each other in the hall every day and we could meet up for lunch and spend a little time together after school. I needed to get her a necklace or a ring or something, now she said she'd be my girlfriend.

I yawned as sleep started to pull me into the night. Maybe I could get to a store this weekend, get her something nice. I still had some of the money from the ATM, part of what we got against Mama's card. But that had to be paid back sometime. I yawned again and settled into my pillow.

I'd figure it out.

Thursday: Beginnings & Endings

-91-

"Are you sure it's okay for me to leave before the healthcare person gets here?" I asked.

Grandpa motioned for me to get going. "Go on, you'll be late. It's only a half hour. He's coming in early so we can get the kids to their schools and get them registered. He'll take extra time at lunch. I don't need to be hovered over the whole day."

"I could drop my first class."

"No. Go. After today, Jake's mother has it all under control. You know that."

We'd figured it all out last night after dinner.

There was a group of parents who took turns watching all their kids starting at seven. They walked them to school as a group, so Jimmy wouldn't complain about being treated like a baby anymore. After school, the healthcare guy would pick up Missy while Jimmy would go to soccer practice with Jake and get a ride home with his mother.

It was strange not to be needed, but it was good that I didn't have to drop my first class. I was already on a short day because I'd been getting out early to walk the kids home. We started doing that last year when Mama still had her job, and we'd never changed it. Now I knew it was to protect the kids from Lester.

Too bad we hadn't had neighbors like the ones here back then. Now summer school was a definite part of my future to make up the credits. I should have gone last summer, too.

"Wait a minute," Grandpa called as I started out the door. "I almost forgot to give you money for lunch."

"We get free lunch," I said. "With you being retired, we probably still qualify. I don't think owning your house counts against it."

"Oh," he said. "I'll have to find out about that when we register Jimmy and Missy."

He didn't look like he liked the idea.

Missy and Jimmy were ready and waiting for the health aide to arrive so they could get going.

"Should we get in the car?" asked Jimmy.

"No, we'll be going in his vehicle," said Grandpa.

"Did you used to have a dog?" asked Jimmy. "There's a couple kennels up on top of the cupboards in the garage."

"We brought two dogs out here with us, but they were old and didn't last long after the move. Angelina kept thinking we'd find Michael and your mother, and that they'd either have a dog or he could pick one out."

"We can get a puppy?" Jimmy exclaimed.

"No!" Missy stomped her foot. "It would hurt the cat, if it comes back to stay."

Grandpa laughed. "We always had cats and dogs. A good cat won't put up with any nonsense from a dog. A good dog will protect his cat from other dogs."

"Really?" she asked.

"Absolutely, but let's wait until I'm back on my feet and steady. I wouldn't want to trip over a puppy and hurt it. But if that cat doesn't show up soon, we could go to the Humane Society and see what kittens they've got."

"You wouldn't trip over a kitten and hurt it?" Missy worried.

"They're better at getting out of the way."

-93-

Lester cursed. There were too many people coming and going to be able to approach the house from the front in the morning, and now some guy had arrived in a van and the old man and kids were getting into it.

Lester pulled down the street slowly to watch which direction they went when they came out of the cul-de-sac, then he turned around in a driveway and followed them, staying well back.

They all went into a primary school first. Not a kid over four feet tall. They were in there a long time and came out without the little girl. When they went to another school a couple blocks away, Lester realized what they were doing. He'd watch the girl's school from two o'clock on. She wouldn't get out earlier than that, and the older kid had gotten on the Light Rail, headed back to the old neighborhood. Didn't take a genius to realize he wasn't leaving his old school. Maybe they were secure enough here that they'd let her walk home.

I was starting to tackle my back assignments when Shenia found me in the school library, half hidden by a pile of books.

"Sorry I couldn't eat lunch with you. They want everything done before next Friday," I moaned. "That includes two major reports and an English paper."

"We should have checked for your assignments when I got mine at home," she said. "Sorry."

"They really post them online?"

"Most of the teachers. You should have a computer."

"I need to learn how to use them better. The paper for English is what's really got me worried. It's a big chunk of the grade and I'd been putting off the research part to the last minute. Now I'm supposed to be revising my rough draft!"

"You get started on the rest. Give me your English topic and I'll pull together some resources for you as soon as my last class is done."

"Really?"

She smiled. "How long can you stay after school?"

"I want to catch the Light Rail by three thirty, so I'm sure I'll get back to the house before the healthcare guy leaves. Just in case, you know?"

"That should give me time to find some books and print out some information from online. I'll call Daddy. Maybe I could go with you and help make dinner, and then we could organize whatever resources I've dug up for that paper."

This wasn't the right place to tell her everything I was feeling, so I tried to put it all into my smile. I think she understood. She smiled back and lowered her eyes almost like she was shy.

"I'll be back right after class," she said.

She headed out of the library. I kept smiling at her until she glanced back and reflected my smile again.

"Please Daddy?"

Shenia's friend waited impatiently for her phone.

"Tell Michael and his grandfather that Schuster says they may have found Lester's sister," her father said. "Her car is near a safe house in San Francisco and they're trying to confirm she's staying there."

"So I can go?"

"Yes. I'll take your mother out to dinner and we'll pick you up between eight thirty and nine."

"Thank you, thank you, thank you!"

"Behave."

"I will. Thank you, Daddy."

Her friend grabbed the phone as soon as she closed it.

"You trying to lose my phone?" she complained. "That was too long. Next time, use someone else's or go off campus to call."

-96-

Lester stretched against his car at the river access like any jogger might do. He had the Sierra Club hat he'd found at the thrift shop pulled low over his eyes.

If he came face to face with one of the kids they'd still recognize him, but not from a distance.

A couple walked past on their way to the river with their dog.

"Hello," the woman greeted him.

He focused on his foot, as if really into his stretching and raised a hand in greeting. They never saw his face, and they headed up the river. He tied his jacket at his waist and headed down the trail. The weather was getting nice again. He'd better be able to finish this today or there'd be witnesses to his taking care of the witness.

That guy had gone and picked up the little girl, but the boys weren't home. Maybe they'd let her play in the back by herself. If she'd just come close enough to grab her.

Missy came running downstairs yelling, "The kitty's in the yard!"

She flew past Grandpa and his aide working with the walker.

"Missy!" called Grandpa. "Stop! You'll scare her off."

Missy bounced impatiently in the doorway.

"She's walking back in the strawberries!"

"If it's a tricolor, mostly black, white bib and an orange triangle above one eye, it's my stray," said Grandpa.

"It is!"

Grandpa made it three more feet with the walker to stand by Missy. He nodded for the aide to get his wheelchair.

"You're right," he said in a hushed tone. "It is her. See how her nipples are hanging low?"

"You mean how her belly's floppy?"

"Yes, her belly's floppy." He chuckled quietly. "She's nursing."

"What's that mean?"

"It means she's got kittens somewhere."

"Can I go pet her now?"

Grandpa answered before he sat down in the wheelchair.

"No, we'll stay right here and watch. When she's ready, she'll bring the kittens to eat with her. If you try to find them now, she'll move them and you might never see her again."

"She's going over to the dish."

"After she leaves, you can add some more food. You want to make sure it's never empty."

Missy didn't move. She stood there quietly next to her grandpa watching the cat eat. When the cat was done, she neatly licked a paw to wipe her face, then slipped away through a broken spot in the back fence.

"Can we go look for her kittens?" asked Missy.

"What did I just say about that?"

"That she'll hide them." Missy sighed.

"Be patient. She'll bring them here to eat when they're ready."

-98-

The cat skittered past Lester and hissed.

He watched, but it headed down the trail away from the loose board behind the old guy's house.

Stupid old man.

If he'd let the girl follow the cat, she was little enough to slip through the fence. Lester could have grabbed her and gotten clear out of sight before they came around to look for her. He could hold her face in the water a few minutes, then toss her in the river. It would be a tragic ending to the whole drama. She liked the cat. All he had to do was wait. She'd come close enough to grab her.

He was never going to hook up with a woman with kids again. They were nothing but trouble. Now he sat behind a large rock where he wouldn't be noticed by anyone walking down the trail and he could hear them talking in the backyard.

The older boy was home, with his girlfriend from the sounds of it. Lester almost left. But there was still a chance. Sometimes when more people were around kids got less supervision.

After the health aide left, we had milk and cookies with Missy and Grandpa in the rose garden. It was kind of cool for sitting outside, but the deck was a sheltered area and the sun was shining.

Jimmy was still at soccer practice, and I didn't have to go get him! He had a ride home.

Shenia and Missy took the plates in. Grandpa heaved a big sad sigh and stared at the fountain.

"Are you okay?" I asked him.

"I'm fine. It's just, this is the first time I've eaten out here since I lost your grandmother, that's all. I was thinking how happy she'd be with all of you here."

"You want me to get you a coat, so you can sit out here longer?"

"Why, yes, Michael. I'd like that. Get me the plaid jacket hanging just inside the garage door, would you please?"

I helped him into the soft old jacket that was more like a really heavy shirt.

"This was my father's," he said.

It was hard for me to believe any piece of clothing could be that old. Mama had always complained how our clothes fell apart. I guess things really were made better back in the day. Or maybe we were buying cheap stuff all the time.

"Have Missy bring some cards out here to play with me," he said.

I didn't have to tell her twice. Missy was always pestering someone to play any game with her. Shenia and I started Grandma Angelina's recipe for spaghetti sauce.

"This is easy enough that you won't need the book once you've made it a few times, and you probably won't stick to it exactly, either," said Shenia. "Chop up a clove of garlic, would you? It's on the cutting board."

"Is this whole thing a clove?" I asked.

"No!" She laughed. "Break off one section. That's a clove. Put in the whole thing and no one would be able to eat it."

"Good thing you're here."

Aside from that the recipe was easy to understand. Fifteen minutes later, a big pot of sauce was on the burner.

"That'll be plenty for a few meals, won't it?" I asked.

"At least three, even with me here tonight," said Shenia. "Put it down on simmer and let it cook until dinnertime. We'll wait until then to make the spaghetti itself. That's simple. The bread you can do however you like it."

"I've done noodles and garlic bread before," I told her.

She gave me a quick kiss, then we sat down at the dining table and she showed me all the research she'd found for my English paper.

-100-

Lester watched through a knothole. The old man was playing cards with the little girl.

Maybe he'd have to go in after her.

He went back to the broken board and started pulling on the one next to it, wiggling it like a loose tooth, a little at a time, gently and very quietly. He almost missed hearing it.

"Here, kitty kitty kitty," called Missy softly.

The girl was approaching the fence, looking for the cat.

Come on kid, three more feet, two… Just one more step…

"Missy, what did I tell you about bothering the cat?" the old man called. "Come finish our game."

The girl ran back to the house.

"I think I can get a good rough draft out of it now. Thanks," I said. "There's no way I'd ever have pulled this much together. I really need to learn how to use computers better."

"You will." Shenia smiled.

We went outside. They were playing Crazy Eights and Missy was winning. She asked if we wanted to play, too.

Grandpa answered for us. "They need some time to themselves."

"Are they going to kiss?" Missy giggled.

"They might. So they should go take a walk outside," he said.

"I don't know..." I said, looking at Missy.

"Thirty minutes," Grandpa said. "You have a watch?"

"We have Michael's cell phone." Shenia was all for it.

I was still worried, though. "Are you sure you'll be okay if we take a walk? Just you and Missy here?"

"I'm not completely helpless, you know."

"No, but you can't move very fast yet, so how about I bring your phone out here while we're gone?" I asked.

He nodded. "That's a sensible precaution."

I got it and put it on the table, then stood there, not leaving.

"We could sit on the bench behind the house," Shenia suggested.

"Listen!" Grandpa sounded angry. "The *biggest* reason I didn't come home sooner was fear. Fear I'd fall again and lie in that house alone until I died of dehydration because no one knew I was hurt."

"Well, that could have happened," I said.

"I was going to die in that place, like Jones, because I was afraid to come home and die alone. And it would have been sooner, not later. I will not live the rest of my life in fear and I won't have my grandchildren living that way either!"

"But..." I stopped myself before I said the name.

"That man may never get caught. We don't have to be stupid, but no one is going to bother Missy here in our own yard." Grandpa slammed his palm down on the table. "Now get out of here. Go take a walk. Be teenagers."

-102-

Thirty minutes. He'd have to go in after her. But not from the back fence, not while the old man had a phone next to him. They'd see him coming.

Lester headed down river to the empty house where he'd spent the night. He'd have to risk going in from the front. They'd think it was the kid and his girlfriend coming back early.

It wouldn't look like an accident, but it could seem to be a random burglary. He could steal something obvious. It would look like he got interrupted. He'd take care of the girl first. The old guy wouldn't be able to get away.

He pulled gloves out of his coat pocket.

103

We headed down the street in silence. My hands were stuffed in my hoody pockets. It was only after we got to the river access that I relaxed. My hands came out of my jeans and the one closest to Shenia reached out and took hers. We walked to the river trail like that and stood watching the water flow past.

"Thanks for suggesting we could sit in the backyard," I said.

"Well, he's right you can't let fear rule your life, but you're right that he's in no shape to protect Missy. But Lester's probably out of state, never to be seen again."

"And there's no way he'd find us here anyway."

"So they're probably fine." She squeezed my hand gently.

"But we won't take too long of a walk."

"Actually," she said slyly, "We could walk down to where you saw your grandpa's fence before, and find a cozy spot to sit awhile."

So we walked down the river trail toward Grandpa's house.

There were lots of board fences. I was looking for his broken board when Shenia spotted the cat lapping water at the edge of the river.

"Quiet," she whispered. "We can watch where she goes."

We stood there motionless as the cat took her time at the river, then gingerly made her way back toward the trail. She was almost to it when she froze with one paw in the air.

She stood like that for at least a minute, then pounced, and we heard a high-pitched squeaking. She lifted her head with a mouse in her mouth, trotted across the path, through some taller grass, and then disappeared through the fence.

"That's the broken board," I whispered. "Grandpa's fence."

"She must have moved her kittens into his yard," whispered Shenia. "We'll have to look for them when we go back."

"We'll have a hard time keeping Missy away from them."

"Is that her laughing?" asked Shenia.

If Missy had been playing with friends behind the house, we'd have heard her loud and clear, but since she was in the side yard playing with Grandpa, I had to listen carefully.

"Yeah, that's her," I decided.

We had been talking in hushed tones for the cat, but now it was so Grandpa and Missy wouldn't know we were so close. We didn't even have to talk about it. We both knew he'd feel bad. It would be as if we didn't trust him to take care of Missy.

"We could sit on that little grassy patch." Shenia pointed to a sunny spot close to the fence.

It was warm enough to take off my hoody and spread it out for us to sit on.

"Thank you." Shenia didn't really need help to sit down, but when I offered it, she took my hand all ladylike. The hoody was small enough that it was natural to sit close with my hand on the ground behind her.

She leaned back against that arm and turned toward me. "Do you really have to change schools? I'll miss seeing you every day."

"I should." The scent of her filled me.

We were staring into each other's eyes, neither of us breathing, leaning closer and closer until finally our heads tilted a little opposite ways and our mouths met and our eyes closed and the world fell away.

I'm not sure how long we were lost in our kissing, pressing up against each other, the heat rising between us.

I do know what made us stop, though.

It was Missy screaming.

104

That fence was built with the smooth side out, but that wasn't about to stop me. There was a big rock near it. I pushed up off that. My waist was strained at the top of the fence and my feet were scrambling to get some traction. Then Shenia's hands were under them and I was on top of the fence for one moment. As I jumped into Grandpa's yard a man's scream pierced the air.

I pounded around the corner of the house and there they were. Missy was behind Grandpa, who was standing with one hand on the table next to the cards. He held the Louisville Slugger ready to strike again. Curled up on the ground beside him was Lester.

Missy had the phone and was talking to 911.

I walked over to Grandpa, careful to avoid getting in range of a grab from Lester. "Where'd you hit him?"

"One to the gut, then another to the knee cap."

"Want me to stand guard so you can sit down?" I asked.

"The police are already on the way," he said.

"I won't hit him unless he tries to get away," I promised.

He handed me the bat and let himself down into the chair.

I didn't even wish for Lester to give me an excuse. It was good enough to know he was caught. The fact that he was whimpering in pain did help, though.

"Where's your sweatshirt?" Grandpa asked.

"We were sitting on it."

Shenia came around the corner of the house more cautiously than I had. She took in the scene before her. "That him?"

I nodded. "You got over that fence without any help?"

"No, I got hold of that loose board and yanked it right off, then squeezed through. The one next to it had some give, too. We'll have to fix your fence, Mr. Dolan. Sorry about that."

"It needed some work, anyway," he said.

Then the police and EMTs arrived. I was surprised Mr. Brown wasn't with them, but Schuster was. He slapped the handcuffs on Lester as he read him his rights, then let the EMTs put a splint on his leg. Lester didn't say a word except to ask for a lawyer. The

EMTs said he had to go to the hospital first. Schuster made sure one of the uniforms would stay with him.

Once they'd all cleared out, Schuster sat down. "What happened here?"

"I might have hit his knee a little too hard," Grandpa said. "But my granddaughter and I were here alone and I figured I'd only have one good swing before he got his wind back."

"Where were you?" Schuster asked us.

"On the other side of the fence," said Shenia. "Sitting, talking."

"You were supposed to be taking a walk," said Grandpa.

"We did," said Shenia. "Then we stopped where we'd hear if there was a problem."

"We had it under control, didn't we Missy?" said Grandpa.

"Yep," she said.

"How'd you happen to have a baseball bat?" asked Schuster.

"I was telling Missy about it, so she brought it out here for me."

105

Jimmy and Jake got home as Schuster was leaving. Shenia took the kids to get my hoody.

When they were gone, I asked, "Did you really have Missy bring the bat down because you were telling her a story about it?"

"Not exactly," he admitted. "I decided you were right that I wasn't in shape to protect her if the need arose, so I had her get it out of your room. I told her how your mother used it whenever she played baseball, though, so I wasn't really lying."

"Are you okay? You didn't hurt yourself?"

"Once I knocked the wind out of him and he was bent over, I let go of the table long enough to swing at his knees two-handed. The twist left me a little sore right above the hip, but I think it'll go away with heat and ice in rotation."

"What do you use for that?" I asked.

"There's a heating pad in the bathroom closet upstairs and frozen peas work fine for the ice part. Ice first."

I brought out the wheelchair, helped him to his recliner, got him the frozen peas and found the heating pad and plugged it in so he could use whichever he wanted. He leaned back and closed his eyes. I put a light blanket over him, then checked on the sauce.

Shenia had said not to scrape the bottom if it stuck, but it hadn't, so I stirred it and then left it simmering. The wonderful smell made my stomach growl, so I snacked on some chips Grandpa had had us include in the groceries.

The kids came back and we searched the yard for the kittens. They were in the corner farthest from the house, under a bush.

"Remember," I said. "Grandpa said not to touch them or the mother will move them again."

"They're so cute," said Shenia. "They're fun to watch."

The mother cat seemed comfortable with the distance we were keeping, until Missy moved a little closer.

"Missy, you don't want her to take them away. This is a safe place for them."

"I know," she said. She backed off.

"Why don't you kids go upstairs and play while we finish getting dinner ready?" Shenia suggested.

They didn't really want to leave the kittens, but they did.

Shenia and I finished getting dinner ready, cleared my work off the table and set it for dinner. We slipped in some kissing, too.

-106-

Mr. Brown put his cell phone away and spoke to his wife.

"That was Schuster. It's over. Dolan got him with a baseball bat, hard enough that they had to take him for X-rays."

"Is Mike okay? And the children?"

"Everyone is fine, including Shenia."

"Shenia was there?"

"I told her she could go home with Michael after school and stay for dinner, so I could take you out to celebrate when we're done here." He smiled.

"Does she know where we are?"

"No."

"Mr. Brown, Mrs. Brown?" The woman behind the desk cleared her throat. "I don't mean to rush you, but have you finished reading over the contract?"

"Do you have a pen?" asked Brown.

"Are you sure?" his wife asked.

"Yes. I liked it when you made me look at it last summer. I was just being stubborn. We should have done this years ago."

The realtor pointed out each place they had to initial and sign.

"That place has been sitting empty so long, I'm sure that they'll be happy to speed up closing for you," she said. "You are getting a great bargain. It's a wonderful neighborhood."

"We know. It's less than two blocks from some very good friends."

Going Forward

-107-

Swede told me that tough times make you stronger, as long as you don't lie around feeling sorry for yourself. He was right. Everyone has tough times. I'm thinking some of us get most of them out of the way while we're young, that's all. I hope so.

The only thing that could have made Christmas better was if Mama, Swede, and our grandmother had been with us, and actually, it felt as if they *were* there.

Shenia and I exchanged presents Christmas Eve, when we had a few minutes of privacy. She wears the ring I got her all the time.

Christmas morning, the Browns came over from their new house for the day. Missy gave Grandpa his Proud Grandpa hat and he fell asleep wearing it that night. The kids got bikes and helmets and Grandpa floored me by giving me a laptop.

When everything else had been opened, Mr. Brown pulled two envelopes out of his pocket. He gave one to Shenia and the other to me. She opened hers first and started laughing.

"Open it, Michael," she said.

So I did. "Driving school?" I laughed, too.

"It's the basics plus defensive driving techniques," said her mother. "They actually have you practice the skills you need in an emergency."

Grandpa put the wheelchair away before Christmas and the walker's been folded up in the closet since St. Patrick's Day. His father lived into his nineties, so he's planning on seeing all of us grow up. He keeps the kids busy after school, playing games with them after they're done with their homework. He's teaching all of us how to garden. He wants me to get a scholarship, but he says he's got enough stashed away to make sure we all finish college.

Shenia and I finished up the semester at our old school, but the new one's better. Her parents push her to get good grades, too. Her mother wants her to be a lawyer. I think she'll make a good one.

We have a date every Friday night. Of course we have to tell her parents where we're going and what we're doing with whom. We usually go to something happening at school or a movie. I've been going to church with them, mostly for the extra time with Shenia.

We took that driving course together, too, once I got my permit. We're both pretty good at controlling a skid. Grandpa lets me use his truck on condition that I never take Shenia parking in it and I keep my grades up. I do all the maintenance, of course.

We scattered some of Mama's ashes at Tahoe and on the river, where we'd taken Swede's. We took some to San Francisco Bay, too, because she'd always wanted to travel. The last bit we put in that pretty little box Grandpa keeps on his dresser, with her mother.

Oh, and Lester. When his sister found out he'd gotten caught in the act going after Missy, she came back to testify that he'd planned to kill the little girl. As for Mama's murder, they didn't admit the letter we found in the cedar chest into evidence, but he had her key ring. It was in his pocket when he was arrested. Missy testified, too. His lawyer tried to make the jury doubt the little girl understood what she saw; he insisted Mama hadn't been afraid. It was when Missy told them what he did to Betsy that the district attorney's case was locked tight. Between the two convictions, Lester Madden will die in prison.

The stray took off once her kittens were grown. We found homes for all of them except one calico we kept.

She looks like Betsy.

Resources

National Suicide and Crisis Line

Call: 988

chat.988lifeline.org/

chat.988lifeline.org/?lang=es

988lifeline.org/deaf-hard-of-hearing-hearing-loss/

National Runaway Safeline

www.nationalrunawaysafeline.org

800-RUNAWAY (800-786-2929)

National Runaway Chat and Info

www.1800runaway.org

800-RUNAWAY (800-786-2929)

Thank you.

Thank you for reading this book.

Please take a few moments right now, while the story is still resonating, to help others find it.

Amazon's algorithms control book sales – the more reviews and ratings a book gets, the more often it pops up for people to see. The more attention it gets there, the more attention it gets elsewhere and the more likely it will find its way to libraries, too.

So please, review this book on Amazon. You don't have to purchase it there to post a review and/or rate a book. You can copy and paste the same review at Goodreads or other places. A review can be short and simple – "Interesting story." is enough for the review to be counted. Don't forget to give it a star rating.

Review links for *Tough Times*:

www.amazon.com/Tough-Times-Sheri-McGuinn/dp/1942069081

www.goodreads.com/book/show/220619945-tough-times

If you want to do more, you can:

- Talk it up – encourage your friends and your local library or book club to get the book.

- If you do social media, post a picture of you with the book.

If you want to know more, you can check out my website. If you have questions, there's a contact form and I do answer messages.

Thanks. Sheri

www.sherimcguinn.com/books

sherimcguinn.substack.com/

Behind the Story & Acknowledgements

When my father was a kid, there were still signs saying "No Irish need apply." As a "Mick" who grew up in rough surroundings, he used Archie Bunker's vocabulary for people before Archie existed.

By the time I was a teenager, Dad had worked his way up to a top executive position in a major corporation and my mother had talked him into *borrowing money* to own a house in the suburbs. He'd just finished paying off the fifteen-year mortgage when a black family moved in across the street. It was the 1960s and "block-busting" was the term used when the first black family bought a home. Dad thought the neighborhood would decay and he'd lose the largest investment he'd ever made. When a neighbor said her friends would like to buy the house for twice what he'd paid fifteen years earlier, we moved to the farm and I graduated from the same small-town school my parents had attended.

Dad probably never knew I'd walked to school with the boy in that house one day. He was a year ahead of me and friends with the boy who'd moved out. We both had the same French teacher. He was a very middle class boy – the only difference was his skin color. In the small town, I was not supposed to date Italian boys.

As years passed, I ran into Italian men who asked after Dad and spoke fondly of how he taught them how to play basketball at the YMCA. I realized he had always looked on people as individuals. His prejudice was class-based, born of his own struggle to move up from poverty. Eventually, he welcomed a Sicilian into the family.

As my kids grew, they had friends of multiple ethnicities, all of them pretty much middle class. I taught in small town, city, and reservation schools. They all inspired Michael because they showed me environment and situation molds people far more than any large label – and family dynamics more than anything else.

Michael's a middle-class kid dealing with one major traumatic event after another. His racial heritage complicates things, but he's been brought up comfortable with himself, so it's not a core issue.

A posthumous thank you to Dad, the inspiration for Michael's grandfather, and to Fred Foote, who read the book and assured me I hadn't stuck my white foot into it too badly writing about this boy.

Also by Sheri McGuinn

Running Away: Maggie's Story

Maggie is already in another state when they realize she's gone. Her mother's missing journal is their only clue. While Peg races to find her daughter before she's hurt or disappears forever, Maggie finds herself in dangerous company. Told in both voices, this is a stand-alone story, yet companion to *Peg's Story: Detours*.

Peg's Story: Detours

A novel that reads like memoir; one woman's journey. Asked for by readers of *Running Away*, this is the full story of Maggie's mother.

"In some ways, the novel is a brutal cautionary tale, showing how one mistake can spiral into a life-changing series of events. In another, however, it is a moving coming-of-age narrative about a girl who discovers herself amid extreme circumstances. A nuanced yet plainly told novel. " *Kirkus Reviews*

All for One: Love, War, & Ghosts

Youthful decisions changed the course of their lives and estranged lifelong friends. Decades later they think they've put 'Nam and PTSD behind them, until the past shoves its way into the present, bringing fear and uncertainty. By the end of the deadly month, their lives again change forever.

Alice

Thirteen-year-old Nina narrates the story of her mother, Alice, who has always been responsible, proper, and totally uptight. The school eliminates Alice's teaching position, then her hippie father drops into their lives, and then the bank sends a letter threatening their home – and Nina suddenly sees another side to her mother.

Discussion Questions

1. How has Michael's mother changed since Swede's death? Who does she have for support?
2. Michael has a strong sense of responsibility and what is right. Where did he get that from? Nature or nurture?
3. Shenia takes charge while Michael and the kids are in shock. What would have happened if she hadn't been there?
4. Michael is responsible for his younger siblings, but we also see that Jimmy is resourceful. When Michael decides to follow Jimmy's suggestion and swap plates, what is his conflict?
5. What do you think of Michael's reaction to flying off the road? His reaching out for help?
6. What do Michael and his grandfather have in common besides the name?
7. Michael's grandfather feels guilty about throwing out Michael's stocking. Why and how has guilt effected his life?
8. Michael has always believed it's his fault his grandparents disowned his mother. Was it really all about race?
9. Has Michael encountered problems because he's biracial? How much does it rule his life?
10. Michael is not technically savvy. In 2012 the author still had students with limited access at home who dealt with it like Michael, by avoiding computers at school. If the story was moved up to today, would that be an issue for any kid? How does trying to hide lack of this skill work against Michael?
11. Shenia's parents have had some rought times, too. Her mother has blamed the neighborhood for their son getting into trouble. Is that reasonable? What difference does a neighborhood make? Why?
12. Lester's sister put him into jail once, now she's helping him. Why? How could the system be improved?

My website has:

Supplemental Materials

Puchasing Links

A Contact Form (ask questions or set up an author visit)

Media Resources

www.sherimcguinn.com

My newsletter caters to readers and writers:

sherimcguinn.substack.com

Review links for *Tough Times*:

www.amazon.com/Tough-Times-Sheri-McGuinn/dp/1942069081

www.goodreads.com/book/show/220619945-tough-times

Every review helps.

Thank you for reading!

www.ingramcontent.com/pod-product-compliance
Lightning Source LLC
Chambersburg PA
CBHW031320170626
46807CB00002B/494